W9-CDV-513

My Escapee

My Escapee

Stories

Corinna Vallianatos

University of Massachusetts Press
Amherst & Boston

This book is the winner of the
2011 Grace Paley Prize for Short Fiction.
The Association of Writers & Writing Programs,
which sponsors the award, is a national nonprofit organization
dedicated to serving American letters, writers, and
programs of writing. Its headquarters are at
George Mason University, Fairfax, Virginia, and its
website is www.awpwriter.org.

Printed in the United States of America

LC 2012025912
ISBN 978-1-55849-986-7

Designed by Sally Nichols
Set in Perpetua
Printed and bound by Thomson-Shore, Inc.

Library of Congress Cataloging-in-Publication Data

Vallianatos, Corinna.
My escapee : stories / by Corinna Vallianatos.
p. cm. — (Winner of the 2011 Grace Paley Prize in short fiction)
ISBN 978-1-55849-986-7 (cloth : alk. paper) 1. Women—Fiction. 2. Women—Psychology—Fiction. I. Title.
PS3622.A48M9 2012
813'.6—dc22
2012025912

British Library Cataloguing in Publication data are available.

The Grace Paley Prize in Short Fiction is made possible
by the generous support of Amazon.com.

For Kevin, for Ellis

Contents

My Escapee

My Escapee

I do not know where Margaret is. She sends me a brochure describing a cruise to the Galapagos, on the back of which she's written, *Shall we pack?* But I can't travel anymore. I have caretakers. In my eighty-eight years, I have never been with a man.

When we were young, Margaret and I flew in a small airplane over the red mountains of Afghanistan. She had red hair then, too. It sprang rowdily from her leather helmet. We didn't need men, we had our permeable selves. The humped mountains were as intimate as a tangled blanket on a bed. I knew that if the plane were to sputter and sink I would accept it, the softness below us made it possible, even tempting.

Now I'm terrified of death. It's everywhere in this rest home, woven into the pattern of the wallpaper, the jellied peach paisleys. The carpets are vacuumed multiple times daily. There is something obliterating about such cleanliness! My caretakers are Carla, a nurse who delivers baby aspirin, vitamin E, and Margaret's missives to me on a domed plastic tray; and Fellow, my nephew, who takes me to his home for lunch, or on other excursions. He calls me Aunt Ginny. "My name is Genevieve," I tell him again and again. "I would like a martini, and salted nuts in the bowl that came to be in our possession so graciously."

Why does this make him laugh? The bowl belonged to a little girl who sold lemonade in my and Margaret's neighborhood on the Cape. She kept mint sprigs in it. One day, Margaret bought the whole pitcher from her because the poor thing had been outside in the hot sun for hours without a single customer. She insisted on giving Margaret the bowl in return. Some might say a child is not to be trusted with a decision like that, but Margaret accepted her gift. It is a pretty little blue-tinted bowl. Fellow says he doesn't have it. I suppose he broke it out of some clumsiness.

Living a long time solves only one of life's mysteries, and that is what it is like to be very old. But even at eighty-eight, there are more years to be had. I admit I grasp for them. A runniness as of uncooked eggs in the neck and breasts, a tentativeness toward food, a dislike of the cinema—this is what I once imagined of my eighth decade. In reality, it has been confusing. Fellow tells me I began wandering, that Margaret was helpless to stop me. I suspect I was simply bird-watching, tracking cries and calls. Wandering purposeful and wondrous, like the great poets. It doesn't matter. Margaret is elsewhere. We lived and laughed and cooked together and slept in twin beds in the same cool room, and now I can't make out the postmark on her letters.

The rest home is in Yellow Springs, Ohio. I went to college here, as did Fellow, who lives here still. We sit on a bench downtown and watch the children (really, college students) stroll by. I am amazed. Women who live with other women now do their very best to look like men. Some of them are cute in a rumpled way, with their Buddy Holly eyeglasses and porkpie hats, but for the most part they are terribly unappealing. Of course, they don't care what my ogling eyes tell them. Or notice that I am ogling at all. I am only a figure in a maroon windbreaker, sitting folded up on a park bench, dissolving into the daylight. (Accompanied by Fellow, a square-faced middle-aged man, which makes me even more invisible.) I want to tell them what they are throwing away. The flowering pubis, the stems their legs. Beauty that could change their lives. They will find out one day.

Margaret possessed the most magnificent clavicles, the left of which was broken at birth and healed on its own.

Still, I imagine that beneath the flannel and military trousers of these young ladies there might be something pleasing, and that imagining occupies me. Does my mouth gape? Fellow interrupts my reverie.

"Aunt Ginny," he says, "tell me about—" and he lists some inane feature of the town. *Oh, the changes time wreaks* is what he wants me to say in a voice scored with cracks. I have noticed that the younger generation derives an odd satisfaction in listening to their elders bemoan such things, when more often than not the elders have brought about the changes themselves.

This time he asks about the Tastee Freeze. "Were cows really kept out back?"

"It was out back I was kissed for the first time."

He doesn't want to hear this. His face draws pleasantly closed and he begins transporting muffin crumbs from his lap to his mouth with a moistened finger.

I reach for the memory. Mouth sodden with lipstick,

ruffled blouse wrenched loose from the waistband of my skirt. Sweet instigator.

"What *was* the good girl's name. We were reading poetry together. Sappho. *What I, in my heart's madness, most desire . . .*" Fellow is staring at his feet, but I don't want to be ignored. What is secret might simply disappear. "When we were done, we fed each other malts with long silver spoons," I say.

"It sounds very spirited. There was a lot of fellowship then, wasn't there, Aunt Ginny?"

"Antioch College was a serious place."

"Oh, I know." He gestures at the undergraduates shambling past us three abreast, rubbing waist fat, their belts studded like dog collars. "I wish I could shield you from this." He thinks I can't take knowing what the college has become, that it's plummeted in the ratings, the alumnae no longer distinguished, and in truth, it used to bother me. When I said something about it to Margaret she replied, "Let the kids riot." I wish they could do so more becomingly.

Fellow looks at his watch. "We'd better get you back!"

We walk down Xenia Avenue, past shops that sell Peruvian shawls and Guatemalan coffee beans and German sandals. I press my forehead up against the glass windows: the shawls are spread like wings, the bags of coffee beans filled to spilling, the sandals posed as if about to take a step. Everything changed by the motion it purportedly makes. Everything gaudy and graceful. I think about finding these objects in their place of origin, picking them up and handling them carefully, even tenderly, and deciding not to buy them because being in their country was enough. But here in Ohio buying them is all you can do.

The front doors of the rest home glide open at my approach. Carla reminds me, with an extended finger, which hallway to turn down to get to my room. My bed is made with a scratchy rose-colored comforter and two flat, perfunctory pillows. People think the old and infirm won't notice—that all we need is a predecessor to a coffin. I lie down. Perhaps they are right.

My nephew's a bachelor. I have recently become single again. He says he gave Margaret a choice: she could either stay in our house on the Cape, or join me in a double room here. But I think she's somewhere else entirely, perhaps traveling again. We traveled a lot in our sixty-three years together. It was a way of creating the proper environment for Margaret, who chafed against routine. She was at her best with someone else's scenery speeding past her, past the rough reflection of her own face.

From the room next door comes a thump and a wail. It is Jean Pritchard, who has likely stepped on the hem of her robe and toppled to the floor. She rooms with her husband, Marty. I burrow under the comforter and place a pillow over my ear. My hearing is still keen, and I don't want to have to listen to Marty's soft encouragement and Jean's answering frustration. I see them in the dining hall, she staring into her bowl of cereal, he squinting through trifocals at the local paper. There is something terribly melancholy about married couples here together. Their quarrels and disregard of each other are on display; they have no privacy. No, I'm glad Margaret chose differently.

I've been here for a summer. It's September now, I believe. When was the last time she touched me? A night in April when I woke to her sitting on the edge of my bed? Her face so close it was unobservable? She was not gentle. She never was. Once, long ago, after our exertions, she noticed a few spots of menstrual blood on her violet silk sheets and incinerated something of mine in retaliation. It was a little tasseled dance program from Antioch in which there were penciled names of all my young suitors, none of whom, obviously, had much impressed me.

I hit the call button. In a moment, Carla comes in.

"Can I get something for you?"

I shake my head quickly.

"Is that a 'no,' or a 'I don't remember what I needed'?"

"The latter."

She straightens my pillow. "Well, you can tell yourself that if you don't remember, it probably wasn't very important," she says.

I suspect it is just the opposite.

The next envelope from Margaret contains a patch of flowered blue cotton. The flowers have three petals and stumpy curved stems like commas. The attached note says, *From your very favorite dress. Do you remember where you wore it?*

She's testing me. I sniff the cloth and run it along my cheek. I remove my dungarees, which exactly match the color of the patch. Then, in my underwear, whose crotch cradles a pad for little leaks, I fetch my sewing kit from the closet. Yes, leaks, but they *are* little. I'm sitting cross-legged on the ground sewing the patch onto my pants when Fellow walks in.

"Aunt Ginny," he says loudly.

If I had poked myself, Fellow would have taken my sewing kit just as he confiscated, at the very first red nick, a beautiful set of steak knives with marbled handles that I used to peel apples. Luckily I haven't.

"Hello, nephew." Why must he stare so? His emotions are not agile. They are slow, leaden, unbecoming. I resist comparing now with then, but in my day people certainly knew how to be more tactful.

"Isn't there someone here who can mend things for you?" he asks.

"I'm doing a little decorative work."

He opens a dresser drawer and rummages in my clothing. "Please dress yourself," he says, tossing a pair of plaid slacks at me.

First, I must remove my belt from the dungarees, which I do waveringly. "Do you know what I read in the newspaper today?" I ask. "In Rio de Janeiro, women have just won the right to single-sex subway cars. They'd had enough of being groped."

Fellow sighs and stoops to help me with the belt, which has become entangled in my pants loops, sly thing.

"Have you ever groped someone?" I ask.

"Of course not," he says, yanking. The belt whips free. It is made of some purposeful fake substance.

"You can tell me."

"Okay. Yes. I used to be a terrible groper. I groped on elevators, in the hallways leading to restrooms, on small aircraft."

"Really?" I say, stunned.

"I groped students, students' significant others, faculty, janitorial staff. I'm so relieved to finally admit it," he says.

He doesn't look relieved. He's smiling stupidly. "When did you stop?" I ask.

"I'm just joking, Aunt Ginny."

"Because you ought to. Stolen touch is hardly touch at all."

"*Joking,* Aunt Ginny. Remember jokes?"

He is offering me something complicated, something I don't want. I avert my gaze, pick up a bottle of perfume from the dresser, spray a little on my wrists.

Fellow says, "That's deodorant. It goes here."

He touches his armpits. I put the bottle down. Toiletries will cross me again and again. A fine white ribbon wrapped round a spool in a little case, for instance. When I tied it in my hair, Carla told me it was for my teeth. It had been hard to handle, slippery, and I'd not managed to make a bow but was fond of the result, anyway. Someone else stared back at me from the mirror that day, someone with a flair for herself.

"Let's say hello to Algebra," I suggest.

We find the cat sleeping in a sunny spot in the lobby, right where it would be easy to trip over her. She's supposed to hop on residents' beds and allow herself to be stroked—thereby lowering blood pressure, slowing the hammering of an unhealthy heart—whenever anyone slurs "kitty-kitty" at her. In reality, she dozes in the lobby all day long, then escapes outside to hunt for chipmunks at night. She shirks her therapeutic duties. I suppose there would be less general respect for her if she didn't.

I sit on the carpet next to her and coax her into standing on her hind legs, front paws folded limply against her chest like a dog begging for a bone.

"That doesn't look right," Fellow says.

I need to think about the scrap of cloth Margaret sent to me. I need a cup of coffee and a table on which to prop my elbows.

Once, I had enjoyed café society, glare of mahogany, svelte sipping figures, intentions hidden beneath other, lesser intentions . . .

"If you'll excuse me," I say.

He waves good-bye. Only when he's turned away do I allow myself to imagine his large hands reaching out to prod and pinch, to rip off something that's not his. "Scat," I tell Algebra. The cat arches her back and makes a mewing sound, a protestation.

In the dining room, the tables have been pushed to one side and a member of the kitchen staff is mopping the floor. She is young but not too young, and her face possesses the stubborn vulnerability of a person engaged in physical labor. She turns, bends, and I can see the V shape of her underwear. I wonder what color it is. Something pale and precious, no doubt. Quit, run, there are other places where you can do other things! I want to call out to her, but she would just stare at me as if I were raving. Someone else brings coffee and a bib to me, and although a biscotti would have been more welcome, again I hold my tongue. There is never anything to say until it's the wrong time to say anything.

But I must concentrate. The scrap. The dress. Could I have worn it to the governor's mansion the time Margaret was honored for cleaning up all those sand dunes? And I spilled my drink on a Louis XV wing chair? Or to the new seafood place in Wellfleet on a Friday evening when we felt a little festive? And the cook's cigarette smoke floated out of the kitchen? Or to Rosa, our housekeeper's, graduation? And I suffered an attack of indigestion and missed most of the ceremony?

Any of the above.

A few weeks later, a box arrives. I hold it on my lap. Margaret must have taken out her dentures to pack it. They bothered her, and whenever she did anything that required any concentration, she deposited them on a tabletop or a sofa cushion, not bothering to place them in a cup. Miraculously, she never lost them, though of course she was trying to. Once, in a bookstore in Athens, I saw her tear a page from an Agatha Christie novel, rip it into little strips, and line her dentures with it.

When she turned forty, she stopped shaving her legs. At fifty, she let the hourglass shape of her pubic hair grow out. Her sixties brought the dentures. Every now and then a new wart, pink as modeling clay, sprouted from her cheek or chin. None of this bothered me. I always thought she was beautiful. The process of her aging was better known to me than it would have been to a husband, and I was sympathetic to it. It was as if she were playing a little tune on a piano, and as she played each of her fingers slipped down one key and began to make a clamorous, still familiar sound.

I remain mostly physically intact. Compressed, a wary kernel.

"Are you going to open it?" Carla asks, interrupting my daydream. She's delivered the box to me, and stayed to tidy up the bathroom.

"I'd like to go outside," I say.

"Fresh air's scheduled in an hour."

"I can't wait an hour." I gesture around me. The carpet nearly matches the comforter, but doesn't. The blank television screen threatens to explode at the touch of a button with laughter and dancing.

"All right. Briefly."

Outside, I can feel soft needles of sunlight entering my skin. Eight or nine unicycles rest against the side of the building, their seats no larger than the rubber clutches of some canes.

"Oh, the children are visiting!" Carla says.

I'm supposed to be excited by this. The children are a band, a troupe that rides around town on unicycles, hair trailing behind them. They're taught how to ride the unicycle at a local preschool, which starts them off on mattresses at age three. Though they never fall, they might, and this endows them with a terrible forward motion no matter how graceful their pedaling may be. They make me nervous, but other people seem to love them. In her haste to see the children, Carla runs back inside without me. I glance around, tuck the box under my arm, and set off across the parking lot. A straggler, a pale boy, cycles up to me. He extends his arms for balance, rotating forward and back, forward and back.

"Miss Genevieve," he says, "where are you going?"

"Be careful, for god's sake. Concentrate. How do you know my name?"

"Because I visit you. A lot."

Unwanted visitor, forgotten visitor, a figure slumped in light . . .

"Little boy, if you tattle on me I'll pop your wheels."

"Wheel," he says, pointing beneath him.

I keep going, crossing a road and passing houses filled with families. Couples holding hands. Mothers pushing babies in strollers. To observe alone the configurations that people make is to experience a liberating kind of loneliness. To not know where you are simply exacerbates this loneliness, buffs it to a shine. Perhaps I'm the only person on earth, I think. Perhaps no one else really exists in proper human form. Only this puzzlement can be real.

Locating the bench where I sat with Fellow is trickier than I anticipated, so I settle for the edge of someone's lawn. After many tries, I sever the tape on the box with my pinky nail. Inside, beneath a mound of *Cape Codder*s (how nice to see that stodgy print again), is a china doll dressed in a lank yellow pinafore. Her name is Greta. She is the one possession from my childhood that's survived, and I used to display her in my and Margaret's bedroom, propping her in a nest of pillows to make certain she didn't topple over and bump her head. Margaret couldn't abide this. She thought that by babying Greta I was indulging something infantile in myself. She did not want children. She was in the world, and didn't care how she'd gotten there or whether it was her duty to open that chute, that fleshy pathway, to someone else. Which was fine with me, because if she had wanted children, she'd have run off with a man. I hold Greta in my lap and smooth my hand over her painted-on hair. Long ago I had a cradle to rock her in.

"Ma'am?" A woman wearing a white tunic and a necklace of orange beads is peering at me. "I live here," she says, gesturing behind her. "Is anything wrong?"

"Why, no," I say.

"You're shaking."

"I am?" I look at my hands. They are vibrating wildly.

"Come inside for a moment," she says, helping me to my feet.

I know what she intends to do. Brew tea. I'd rather have sherry.

"I'll just be on my way," I say, stooping to retrieve Greta.

"You could use a change of clothes."

I'm wet. It's the grass's fault. I begin to cry because no one will believe me and then I smell it, the urine, and still I must convince myself it's the grass's fault and the effort of honest deceit is more than I can bear. I follow the woman into her house, sniffling, and tell her that Fellow is my nephew. No one needs last names in a town this small, which is good because I've temporarily forgotten what Fellow's last name is, forgotten my own. I accept a pair of pants which are too large for me, and yes, a cup of tea, and sit at a kitchen table with a very pleasing blunt honeyed grain.

The woman makes a phone call. Then she sits across from me. "Running away?" she asks, smiling.

"Of course not."

"But you *were* in a hurry."

"I was resting," I say.

"You'd tired yourself out."

I clutch at Greta. My nails are bits of dirty glass.

"You see, I don't believe you. You look sad. Lovelorn. Like—" and she demonstrates by frowning and tugging violently at her jowls.

"How rude!"

She takes a quick, wet sip of tea. "I just want to make sure you're being cared for," she says. She waves her hand in a westerly direction. "You're all so willful, you people from over there. Every now and then one of you flies across the street and lands in my yard and I have to take action. Intervene. And you hate me for it. I think you hate me for not being young anymore, myself."

She may be right. I wouldn't put it past us.

There's the sound of car tires on gravel. "Thank goodness," she says as she rises to let Fellow in.

The time for games is over, I write to Margaret on a piece of my stationery. *Stop sending me these puzzle pieces.* Though it appeared from the newspaper protecting Greta that Margaret is still on the Cape, I have, as I've said, my doubts. What would she do alone in our house without anyone to boss around? She probably took that cruise to the Galapagos without me, and this, thinking of her so far away, a distant figure wearing a ridiculous hat (all hats are), emboldens me. *You don't awe me anymore,* I write. *You rather disgust me, and I've met someone else.* Then I throw the stationery away, flop on my bed, and stare out the window. Someone else. At my age, that's a laugh. A long, phlegm-flecked howl.

Carla intercepts me as I'm leaving my room to go watch *Big* in the common area. "Where did you think you were going yesterday?"

"On a little walk."

"A little walk, for someone like you, is a little tragedy."

She's holding an envelope. "I don't want that," I say.

"It's yours."

"It disagrees with me."

"Here," she says.

"Carla," I groan, thrusting the envelope back at her, "not now."

She blinks, and pushes it into my chest again. "You don't have to open it."

I return to my room. The envelope's coming undone at the flap, it's practically opening itself. Inside, there's a sheet of lined notebook paper that says:

> *Fondness for you*
>
> *Pliability*
>
> *Taste in china*
>
> *Delicate wrists*
>
> *Lack of fondness for you*
>
> *You were a distraction*

There is a telephone number written on an index card and taped to the top of the television. I dial it. The receiver is lifted on the other end. "Hello?" someone says.

"Tuesday!" I say.

"Aunt Ginny, you scamp. How did freedom feel?"

"Who is this?" I ask sternly.

"It's Fellow," the voice says, and my brother leaned toward me over a bowl of chowder, happiness making his face a clearer color. What was it he wanted to tell me? The spoon in his hand shook, tim-tim-timmed against the rim of his bowl, and Fellow, he said, he'd named his son Fellow, and then I know who it is, and a mild disappointment comes over me.

"Are you all right?" the voice asks.

"Fine." I have to sit down. It's dizzying, the way the past unfolds in crystal bits, and the present's this faulty plateau. Fellow must be waiting for me to speak.

"Freedom, you say? It didn't feel like it."

"Isn't that often the case," he says.

"Meet me in the lobby," I command, and hang up.

A crowd of white heads rings a black blot on the lobby floor. It's Algebra, who's decided to die where she usually naps. Everything about her is furry and defenseless. Maybe that's why she wasn't so interested in hopping on residents' beds and being patted, I think. Maybe she was old, like us, and could have used her own pet to pat.

The crowd murmurs. A few people sob. When an aide comes and scoops Algebra up, someone collapses. It's Jean Pritchard.

I kneel at her side. "Don't pretend you loved that cat."

Marty kneels next to me. "She loved the thought of her. She truly did."

I pat Jean's face. Her eyes open in time for her to see Algebra being carried from the room, paw swinging like the softest pendulum. The aide turns the corner and the cat disappears. I feel a stabbing in my stomach. I'd rub my thumb and index finger together and sometimes, only sometimes, would she rear up toward me. She possessed a grand indifference.

"Are you the crazy lady who lives next door to me?" Jean asks.

"I am," I say proudly. I wish Margaret could hear me.

"It hardly seems you're there. So quiet, no TV."

"I pass the time. Think of the face of someone you used to love. Not him." I nod at Marty. "If you haven't seen this person for a long time, age him. Scar him, wrinkle him, weaken him. Trap him in your room. Make yourself his only hope."

"Visualization!" Marty says. Hovering, always hovering. He smells like masking tape.

"Marty," Jean snaps, "butt out of it." She squeezes my arm and looks at me intently. "What if there's only been one?"

"One what?" I ask.

"One person."

I jerk my arm from her grasp. Fellow is threading his way through the crowd, a foot taller than everyone else.

"What happened, Aunt Ginny?"

"Can we sit?" We find a couch on the far side of the room. "We've lost Algebra," I say. His face remains blank. "The cat."

"Oh. Well, I guess it all—"

He pauses, and I can hear the rattling of a cart, the clapping of shoes after it.

"—ends," he says.

"Fellow." I turn to look straight at him. "Where is Margaret?"

"On the Cape." His voice catches, and he clears his throat. "Where else would she be?"

"She's not a prisoner. She could be anywhere!"

"It would be hard for Margaret to be anywhere."

"Is she unwell?" I ask.

He looks away from me. "Ah, Ginny," he says, leaving off the aunt part, and I hear worse than unwell. It's funny how words do that, bend themselves into truer shapes. "A month after you left for Ohio," Fellow says, "Margaret died in her sleep." I hear five phantoms creep. "I was afraid you'd feel it was your departure that did her in." I hear tagged and binned. "So," he says, "when I went to the house on the Cape to take care of things, I collected the odds and ends that Margaret had been intending to send to you." No one knew. "And for the last few months," Fellow says, "I've been mailing them from over in Springfield. They were Margaret's notes, Margaret's handwriting. They were her packages, all set aside for you." He rests his hand on my shoulder. "I know this is very sad."

"Don't touch me," I say.

He snatches it back. “I’m sorry.”

It costs him some effort to rise from the couch. He scoots forward, swivels, pushes off the armrest. His sigh is gladiatorial.

I haven’t been able to really see Margaret since I’ve been here, but now that I know where she is, I can. Not in death, of course. She desired an unexamined ending. But in some of the places along the way.

Afghanistan. After the plane ride, Margaret went into a tent with the pilot for a very long time. She had not yet started to treat me badly, so I suspected nothing. The landscape was cold and marvelous, and I knew that was how I must appear to her, when she emerged.

Madrid. Every café sold potato omelets. We ate so many of them we got sick. Yet when we returned to the Cape, Margaret tried to forbid me from preparing anything else.

Lisbon. We were walking down a street that descended to the edge of the city. There was the sense that we existed outside of things, by choice, not by choice. Our arms were brushing against each other’s, and the street became steps, uneven and rocky, and the tram was coming up the other way. When Margaret tripped quite close to the track, before she managed to steady herself I had the thought that the driver wouldn’t stop for her, that he’d be content to run her down. I readied myself. She caught her balance. My readiness was taken away.

Posthumous Fragments of Veronica Penn

2007. Even now, she could summon the moment that she met her husband, though she didn't often want to. No, she liked to daydream about another young man, whom she could still see—it was uncanny how crisply—walking toward her, his face full of what she'd thought was confidence but later recognized as the irreverent beginnings of love. Saying, "I really should know your name." Veronica, she'd answered, and never had it fit her so well. This was at Grinnell. She remembered the greedy way he kissed and how, after the first time they had sex, he was suddenly hard upon her from behind saying he could go again, but she had long forgotten her own telephone number. Her existence wanted to flow in the opposite direction from where it was heading, from annulment. Her facts, what medicines she was taking, her daughter Jane's email address (written on the top of every page of her wall calendar), the name of her doctor (Pender-almost-like-thunder), so uninteresting. Just data. But this college boyfriend—what was so special about him? She'd known him before she knew herself.

Her husband had died two years earlier and his ashes whisked away to California, where Jane lived, and where he was originally from. Jane had traveled up the coast from her home in Los Angeles to a little town called Cambria, and scattered him. She'd mailed Veronica a picture of the occasion: her standing on a beach with a wooden box in her hands, the wind whipping her hair back to reveal a face scoured clean by intent. Veronica could see she so wanted to do this thing, honor her difficult father by setting him free. She had stared at the picture until the 6:30 news came on, and then thrown it away.

1971. In the medicine cabinet: nail clippers, jar of Oil of Olay, a comb, deodorant, tweezers. She allowed her hair to bang around her face. The dire little wrinkles between her eyes bothered her only slightly. She was thirty-five, wore jeans and clogs, an expression of strident neutrality. She'd had her one child and would have no more, because Jane was all she needed. But are you, she sometimes asked herself, all *she* needs? No, yes, it was amazing how flaccid and disorganized one moment could be, and the next sparking with possibility. Her husband, Franklin, was gone most of the day, teaching history at his sub-par college. Jane was in third grade. Veronica had time to figure out what, exactly, she wanted to do. But she was distracted. Franklin no longer came to her at night. It had been five months, at least. Distracted by absence, as solid as a real thing. She went to work as a book buyer for the local library system. On her desk: paper bag of granola, Jane's kindergarten picture (tender uneven homemade haircut), Jack Finney's *Time and Again* (which she'd read twice already). Telephone. "Do you want me to bring dinner home?" Veronica called Franklin to ask.

"The refrigerator is empty," he said accusingly.

"I'll pick up Chinese." The crowdedness of the road and restaurant lobby made her frantic to get the food, as if there was a great famine and this a rare, fought-for meal. When the man handed her the bags she wanted to cry, confused by the temporary largesse of strangers.

1964. Jane's high chair was crusted with a paste of Cheerios. Veronica stood in front of her daughter, watching her eat. She was fascinated by everything: a straw wrapper, a toilet paper tube, Veronica's wedding ring. She'd have stuffed it all in her mouth if Veronica didn't intervene. Motherhood was lifeguarding ordinary shores. Elation, exhaustion, elation. Jane threw a Cheerio into her hair. Veronica strapped her into her stroller and they walked. Up the streets and down. Others smiled at them but did not speak, afraid of being drawn into something they'd never escape. Jane clapped, squealed. Veronica wondered how she should experience this. It was in the cool air, the ardent leaves of the trees, it was everywhere outside of herself, winning. They went back home and she changed Jane's diaper, and drove to Bloomingdale's to let Jane crawl about on a floor that was surely cleaner than the floor at home. Past the legs of stools on which women sat settling the difference between lipsticks. Through the shadow-paces of shoppers. Time was sludge-slow. A million gestures a day.

1946. The edge of the stream. Sound of birds and woodpeckers, watery rustle of leaves, uneven buzz of insects. Wonderful, really, the plain mystery of what else was right where you were, in the same square foot of air. A wilderness not of your own making, and perfectly suited to you. There'd been a health resort here once, built to harness the healing powers of the springs' high iron content. Now only the foundation of the hotel remained, massive stone pilings that rose from the water like squared teeth, and that Veronica and her brother Julian were in the habit of crossing, despite being told not to. They were secret leapers.

"Try to catch me," Julian said. He whooped off across the stream, arms outstretched. Veronica followed more carefully, stopping to rest along the way. The water was ten or so feet below, blinkingly eddying. Shards of light like tiny hammers, miniature blown sails . . .

He was already crossing back. "It's never a competition with you."

"You're too fast," Veronica said, and that seemed to satisfy him. He hopped onto her piling and they sat down, back to back, letting their legs dangle. The sun made her sleepy and happy. When one of her sandals slipped off and fell into the water, and she limped home half-barefoot and her mother scolded her in a shrill, protracted way that meant the lost shoe was an insult to what was really wrong, she realized she should have just gone ahead and raced him. She realized her carefulness had been for nothing. She lay with Julian on his bedroom floor, stomach growling, unwilling to appeal to the keeper of the kitchen.

"I'll get us something," Julian said, and returned with a bowl of pretzels and two cold bottles of lemon-lime soda. A treat. Their mother's way of saying sorry.

What was really wrong: a life of slavery to four children. (Veronica guessed this.) That her mistakes and the demands her mistakes made (like the need for new sandals) were the most annoying of the bunch, because taking care of a girl was different than taking care of boys. Because she was her mother in miniature. Because boys were distant enough to pity, and prize.

1988. Veronica sat watching the weather report on TV. She had a great need to know what the weather would be like here in Virginia and, just as urgently, in other parts of the country. A nice day for her was gliding about town on errands, walking the dog. A miserable day was a handful of miniature Hershey's bars and a cup of International Coffee, letting the pounds pile on. Ice storms, snow storms, wind and rain. T-storms, condensation. Cloud cover. The language was eerie and inexact. When it was warm here, but cold where someone she knew lived (like Illinois, where her parents remained until they died), she experienced a kind of thrill, a little loving superiority and concern. When it was nice elsewhere (like California, where Jane was), and awful in Virginia, Veronica went to bed early and burrowed under her blankets, picturing her progeny sleeveless. How just that Jane lived in a place with better weather than she. It would be all wrong if it were the opposite. She would worry incessantly about black ice, skidding tires, doomed decisions becoming doomed results. Staring at the weatherman's face was like admiring something for all the wrong reasons. Wet-newspaper skin and lips like internal organs. Glistening, wiggling. They would never put a woman who looked like that on television, obviously. The weatherman extended his pointer to the glowing Mid-Atlantic. White fleece rushed by, and swooping, swirling lines, meant to show wind currents. "A brisk weekend," he intoned, and Veronica shivered under her chenille throw, "followed by a warming trend," and she extended her foot from beneath. Her big toenail had gone yellow at the edges, like a pearl being swallowed up by sickness.

1960. He unloaded the food from his tray: meatloaf, mashed potatoes, green beans, a slice of lemon meringue pie. "Thanks for that," he said, as if they were continuing a conversation, though he'd just asked if he could share her table. The cafeteria was crowded.

"You're welcome," Veronica said. She was wearing linen pants and a peasant blouse embroidered with bluebells. Her hair was long and her face was lean and focused on his pie, as if she were fascinated and compelled by its complexity. She never allowed herself pie.

He noticed her looking. "Would you like some?"

She nodded. He extended the plate to her with its untouched fork. She took a bite, wiped the fork on her napkin, and put it back. The filling was deep and cool, the meringue crackly. She decided that when he asked if she wanted another bite she'd eat the whole piece, charmingly savage. He didn't ask. Instead, he launched into a story about a biology class he'd taken there at the University of Illinois. Each student had been given a dead cat to dissect, and he'd carried his home on a bus.

"It was wrapped in newspaper, but its tail was sticking out. I was stroking it, making purring sounds," he said. She smiled a smile of adjusted expectation, a little chink of emptiness. They exchanged names. He reached his hand across the table and lifted one of the ribbons that fell from the open collar of her blouse, on the end of which was a chunk of turquoise, and tugged at it.

"Can I buy you dinner sometime?" he asked.

She was in library school, surrounded by quiet, gum-chewing women. Occasionally the gum ended up on the books, and then there was a ruckus of self-recrimination. "That would be nice," she said.

"Will you wear a skirt?"

An odd question. Franklin's dark eyes did not leave hers.

"If you want me to," she said.

1949. She and Julian were crouched behind the living room sofa. "Watch," she said. Their parents had been at a dinner party across the street, and now their shoes could be heard on the path that led to the door. She wanted Julian there because she'd seen their mother come home earlier, to check that their younger brothers were sleeping, and she'd been acting strangely. The figures approached the door and their mother walked right into the long rectangular pane of glass beside it. She fell to the ground and started laughing. Their father said something indiscernible, but the laughter was clear. There she sprawled, in her emerald green cocktail dress, legs ajar.

Veronica could picture the expression on her father's face—more an absence of expression, really. He extended his hand to their mother and pulled her to her feet. The doorknob rattled and turned. Veronica hunched into a knot.

". . . makes Marty tolerable," their mother was saying as she came in. "And Lucille just standing there with that look on her face. Like she's gulping down medicine."

"She's quite pretty, though. She has a fine figure," their father said.

Veronica could feel Julian's back tense. "A little pyramidal, perhaps," their mother said. "I'd like another drink." Clink. Glug. The sound of kissing was the sound of darkness. "Pretend I'm Lucille," their mother whispered.

"That's pathetic," their father said.

Julian's back was quivering—was he crying? Trying not to laugh? Veronica's legs were asleep. Four kids, and they all had their own bedrooms. A zipper's nasal undoing. "I'm gone," she practically shrieked into Julian's ear, and they ran for it. Surprised shouts behind them, and then her door closed and locked.

1980. Franklin was teaching at Evergreen State for a year, and Veronica had flown to visit him, allowing Jane—a high school senior—to remain at home by herself. He met Veronica at the airport and took her to his office. Over his desk, *National Geographic* photographs of the small brown breasts of African girls whose smooth faces were utterly unconcerned with their nakedness, and a topless Marilyn Monroe whose smile acknowledged nothing else. It seemed he wanted all sorts of nipples aimed at him as he worked. "Have any of your female students complained?" Veronica asked.

Franklin laughed. "Some males too." He would offend everyone here as he offended everyone everywhere. The hippie sensibility of the place wouldn't save him. Veronica imagined Jane at home, standing in front of the refrigerator, drinking chocolate milk out of a carton. She imagined this was how Jane would spend her freedom.

They went to Franklin's apartment. Beer bottles on the floor next to a fold-out couch, newspapers in ragged piles, an open jar of caramel sauce with a spoon sticking out of it. She had never, in her adulthood, had such a place.

She put down her bag. "This reminds me . . . "

He was opening a window. "Yeah?"

"Of when we met. That boarding house where you lived, how I tried to make it cheerful."

"You sewed curtains, didn't you?"

She started laughing. "That must have been someone else. I wouldn't have known how to do that." Her laughter was turning into crying, as it sometimes did. Franklin had once been a real person. Now she knew him so well he was indefinable. Not husband or best friend or lover. A smudge acting on itself to blur its own outline. A hot whir of color.

He came to stand in front of her, taking both of her hands in his. "You're right, you wouldn't have. But I liked that about you. It made you serious."

"I think I *was* serious," she said.

1991. The tumor was pressing on the part of Julian's brain that controlled speech. "Broken pieces," he'd say, meaning cereal, and "can-water," meaning juice. It was more baroque, if anything, the way he now expressed himself. "Rain-cube" was the bath, and "magic carpet" his bed. "Why a magic carpet, do you think?" Veronica asked their younger brother Avery. They had all gathered at Julian's apartment in Hawaii. There wasn't much time left.

"He's transported while he sleeps?" Avery guessed. "He's always had really vivid dreams."

"Oh, gosh, me too," she said. Her dreams were logistical nightmares of missed planes, the dead zones of cut phone lines, people from the future trying to talk to people from the past through the dirty mouthpieces of space helmets. She felt chatty and panicked. Their youngest brother, Jack, stood at the foot of Julian's bed massaging his feet. Julian was dozing. Veronica decided to go out and buy a lei to place around his neck, so he'd smell it when he woke up. She could just picture it, a loop of purple orchids, fragrantly exhorting him to stay. Its beauty needing a witness.

Their mother was still in Illinois, too averse to travel to have made the long trip. Veronica thought of her while she was in the car, how she seemed never to want to leave her house. Dying was for the brave, for those foolhardy enough to have lived. She found a woman selling leis at an abandoned gas station, the flower necklaces hung from the pumps, and bought six of them, each more colorful than the last. When she returned to Julian's apartment, she slipped them around his wrists, his ankles, his head. Decorating his body for the here-and-now.

1981. It took a second for her eyes to adjust to the darkness of Jane's dorm room. A sheet had been draped over the window, the mattress dragged off its steel frame onto the floor, and there the disconsolate figure of her daughter lay. As she moved toward her, a piece of typing paper half-emerged from a word processor caught Veronica's eye. Quickly, she bent forward; it was an essay on the poetry of someone named Louise Bogan.

"Jane," she said, crouching beside the mattress. "I'm here." Her daughter feigned waking up, unfolding her body from its fetal curl. Her hair was wet at the brow.

"Oh," she said. She used to say this when she was pleased with something, when told there was no school that day, or that she could have a set of vampire teeth. Oh. An affirmation. A charm clipping another charm on its silver chain. Now it was something else. Other words had proved worthless, so *Oh,* she said.

When Veronica gave birth to Jane, she assumed her loveliness would last her whole life. And for a while, it had. But then Jane turned sixteen, and grew depressed and fat. Or perhaps it was the other way. Sadness overlaid loneliness which overlaid the logical reasons for her loneliness (and there were probably many). A shameful memory: Veronica had put her on a scale and told her that she should try to weigh at most 129 pounds. She told her that when *she* was sixteen, she'd not let herself go above 125.

"Let's get you showered," she said. She found Jane's pail of toiletries and accompanied her down the hall to the bathroom. Her daughter stepped out of her underwear as soon as her feet touched tile. The largeness of her body, the unwieldy way it had gotten the best of everything . . . Veronica stood in the fringe-spray of hot water and handed her a fossilized bar of soap. Jane dug under her breasts, under her arms, in her black thatch of pubic hair. Bubbles blossomed from her skin. They did not say anything. The sound of the shower was glorious, prohibitive. Things would work out, surely, but for now it was like Jane was four again and Veronica was overseeing this exciting new way of washing oneself that wasn't a babyish bath. Another girl came in, wrapped in a terrycloth robe. Soon the air was filled with the scent of banana.

1944. Veronica had a great-uncle who was very rich, and who was coming to her parents' house on Rice Road. Her mother had been cleaning for a week, first wearing her absurd cloves-and-cinnamon-sticks apron, then with the apron looped over her head but not tied around her waist, and finally not wearing it at all. Her hands stank of scouring powder and her face of fatigue. Veronica wanted to tell her mother she was making the house nice at her own expense.

"Little girl," her great-uncle said when he finally arrived, "and you, little boy," to her brother, "and you too," to her other brother, "are there any more of you hiding around here?" He looked about in mock alarm.

"Not yet," her mother said. There would, in fact, be

another child very soon, but her great-uncle was choosing not to acknowledge her mother's pregnancy, so her mother, of course, did not mention it.

"Thank goodness," he said. He pulled Julian onto his lap. "Now, I'd like to get each of you a gift, something you've been longing for."

Julian didn't hesitate. "A new baseball glove."

"Splendid," Veronica's great-uncle said, and slanted his legs so that Julian tumbled off. He turned to Avery. "And what would you like?"

"A sled," Avery said, though he was so young the words barely came out. Veronica's great-uncle did not have any children of his own, and Avery, with his padded bottom and preposterously large head, must have seemed an abomination.

"Fine!" he said. He turned to Veronica. "Well, young lady?"

"A trip to Europe," she said. "Thank you."

"Veronica!" Her mother's face was red.

Her great-uncle laughed. "Ah, ha, you can't have *that*."

"Of course not," her mother said quickly, but her uncle wasn't listening. His head was cocked to the side as if an invisible guide were telling him something.

"Europe doesn't allow girls in, you see," he said.

Veronica's heart pounded as she wiped her palms on the pale-yellow skirt of her dress. It was up to her to defend the borders of Europe, to disabuse her great-uncle of his old manish thought. So much he didn't know! The world this possible thing, but to her great-uncle just the opposite.

"Then I'd like to be a boy," she said.

1996. The lamps shone in all shades of yellow, pull chains dangling like earrings against the necks' pale stems. Lamps on tables and lamps on the floor. The whole room a declaration of light. It hardly seemed you could be angry here—could be anything but reminded of your own childhood, perhaps, of reading on the couch while the adults creaked and groaned around you—but apparently Franklin could. He possessed an ambition to be heard. As she moved, bewitched, through the store, heading toward a beautiful lamp with a marble base, he said, "The shades will catch fire. They're cheap. And why aren't you being helped?" He jerked his head toward the proprietor, who was conferring with someone who'd arrived before them. "Ask for help! Pardon me, ma'am!"

Veronica whispered, "Be quiet. You promised." She'd spoken with him earlier, as she was forced to do before all of their errands: prepare him for what was going to happen, wager and beg, qualify and threaten. And though he'd said he wouldn't interfere, here he was being terrible, a minute in.

He thought she couldn't do anything well, that her every idea was driven by gullible need and stupidity. That she was stupid, yes. Thirty-five years of marriage had come to this—he in his basement office, she watching harmless little shows on TV. A shared dinner in front of the news with their old dog Sylvie on the floor in front of them, waiting for scraps. The dog's back to the TV because the TV didn't feed her.

Now he waved his arm and whistled. She felt faint; it was the *injustice* of it. "Hey!" he called, and again, "Shrreeee!"

"Stop it," she hissed, grasping at him, but he laughed and shook her off.

The proprietor approached them, her other customer pretending to examine something. "Can I help you?" She was a youngish woman with a heavy layer of foundation on her face, like a green leaf made up to look orange.

"I'm sorry," Veronica said, and exited the store she'd have happily wandered for an hour if Franklin were not with her.

1984. The best thing she ever did was give birth to her daughter. The worst thing she ever did was allow Perry Lopez to stay over for a week while Franklin was off teaching somewhere again and Jane was in college. Most of her activities fell someplace in between, where there was only commerce and worry and busyness. Jane's birth happened in three swift hours, from the first labor pains to the last wild push. She'd been more confident about that one act than anything else she'd done in her life. Odd that blood should have accompanied it. Perry was someone she'd worked with. He had a soft furry stomach and a penis that he treated with rueful regret. They'd put on *Evita* and listened to Julie Covington sing "Don't Cry for Me, Argentina," and he'd insisted on undressing her using only his teeth. Engaged places on her body that hadn't been disturbed in a decade. The scaly tips of her elbows. The placid inner thigh. They called in sick to work. Nighttime noises made Veronica leap. Why was this the worst thing? Teleported back in time. The loose philosophy of teens without the amnesiac ability. Her guilt surprised her with its staying power.

1991. Franklin tugged the dog's leash. He never gave Sylvie as much time to sniff as Veronica did when she walked her. They turned the corner and saw a woman with straight blonde hair and a baby on her hip looking in the gutter. Even though it would get Franklin involved, Veronica approached her. "Did you lose something?" she asked.

"My earring," the woman said. She lifted a strand of her hair and tilted her head to show Veronica the other, a tiny, strenuously glinting diamond. Then her forehead wrinkled. "Are you Jane Penn's mom? I went to high school with her."

Veronica could tell—the diamond earring, the sleek spill of hair—that she and Jane had probably not been friends. Who had Jane been friends with? There was a Chinese boy named Nathaniel with a skin tag like a lollipop stick growing out of his ear. He'd never said a word to her. It didn't matter. All he'd not said he was saying now, to someone else. The awkward were not usually awkward for life. Jane was a college professor and mother of a young son. In the process of getting a divorce, yes, but that took confidence.

"I am," Veronica said. "What's your name?"

"Elizabeth," the woman said. "Isn't it funny."

Veronica held her baby—who cried and kicked his legs a little—while Elizabeth scoured the sidewalk. At first the baby's cry alarmed her, and then became just a tuneful annoyance. A kind of lullaby.

Franklin called from a few yards away, "Is this what you're looking for?"

Elizabeth hurried to him. "Oh, wow, thank you." She slipped the earring into her pocket and took the baby back on her hip.

"Your precious things," Veronica said. The baby's eyelashes fluttered with nearly sensual relief.

1999. Laundry in the washing machine. Dishes in the sink. Everything had a place where it was, and a place it should be. Dirt on the sills, dun-colored gluey mucus ringing Sylvie's eyes. The dog looked at her, Veronica thought, reproachfully. The fur on her muzzle had gone all white. Easy to read her aging as acquiescence, each day undoing the day before. Franklin was on prostate medication that made him dizzy if he stood up quickly. Veronica's lower abdomen had become a roadmap of veins which bulged softly from beneath her skin. The grass was ragged at the borders of the lawn. The sky threatened complete closure. Dinner was Franklin's fried salmon and sweet potatoes to the staccato roar of the television. There was pleasure in this because it was simple, because she risked no exposure or embarrassment. Franklin cursed at the people on the screen, female newscasters in particular, and no one but Veronica could hear. Auditory head-banging. Vitriol. It offended her, but she was so thankful that she was the only one offended it was nearly okay. After tidying up the kitchen, a special on PBS. A comfortable chair. She wasn't too proud to admit it. There was pleasure in this.

2003. Things that made her sad: a childhood friend who'd gone blind. Sylvie's last gulped meal. The slights Jane used to suffer at the hands of her unthinking friends. Animals in cages. Animals being hunted. A mess of feathers protruding from a cat's mouth. Franklin saying she was hard to love. The time they were fighting and she ripped Jane out of his arms. Animals in impoverished countries. The little dog who lived around the block dying of cancer. Her grandson getting her cards with their twenty-dollar bills and pocketing the cash and throwing the cards away. The sight of her breasts in the mirror. Any animal being unhappy, confused, scared. Tubes or needles. Lab coats. Singing stringent words across the phone line to her daughter. The way they hurt one another. Jane asking how she could not have known she was clinically depressed. Veronica thinking that term was stuff and nonsense. Her brother dying while she slept in his apartment and the ocean whistled outside. Her father and mother dying. The game of jacks, which she used to be so good at. Spilling the little knobby pieces and the ball from their cloth bag. The way the flesh of her fingers bunched up around her rings. The bald faces of neighbors' children come to sell their parents' houses. The brochures for nursing homes she got in the mail. The pallor of the pastels of the nursing homes' walls. Doctors' handwriting. Bath mats with their blooming suction cups. Photo albums, even empty ones.

2008. She wondered more and more what death would be like. Falling asleep? Going under anesthesia? Maybe it would be best in a dentist's chair, her head raised a little. The blandness of the room nothing to covet at the last minute. Some recognizably unrecognizable song playing, and the smell of fillings like hot medicine. The hygienist's touch. "Mrs. Penn? Are you all right?" Her silence.

Anywhere but a bed, particularly a hospital bed. Walking along, window shopping. The stores in Old Town a bit stuffy for her taste: doggie bakeries, hair salons, starchy sailing clothes. The egalitarianism of her midwestern upbringing chafed against this. A carefulness to people . . . so that when she collapsed upon the sidewalk, there'd be a pause before a passerby rushed to her side. Her slack body so untidy.

In a movie. Going to movies alone had become a pleasurable habit in her later years. She would eat her popcorn and subside into non-thought, reacting only to the bold prompts that cinema offered, the beautiful cues. Her dying would go unnoticed—unless she yelped or cried out—until the theater emptied and an employee came in with a dust broom. Poor soul. Would it scar him to find her, or would she become fodder for a tale to tell friends?

At the bank. A man stood outside the bank and opened the door for anyone entering or exiting, all day long and every day, as far as she could tell, for he was always there when she went to deposit a check. This was the sort of man who would attempt CPR on her, no matter how dead she appeared. A half-hero. A volunteer fire fighter, a police academy flunkee. He would pound away at her bony old chest, and a crowd would gather because he wanted one to.

During the act of love. Ridiculous. But it could happen. It had happened to someone out there, surely. A nice thought.

Comforting. But it would be hard for the other person. He would wonder if he'd been too forceful, too violent. Would there be a way of conveying, from the other side, that it wasn't his fault? That her heart had simply given out like a tomato falling from a kitchen counter to the ground?

2008. From the other side: oh, the things she'd tell people! She'd warn them not to honk at your child when she's riding her bike, causing her to fall and break her pinky (oh stupid overeager thing); stick your arm through a ripped screen door to pat a dog that you don't know (emergency room stitches); lie, cheat, be daft or clumsy. But of course she couldn't undo events that had already happened—or she'd undo her own death, wouldn't she? It would have to be future warnings, avoiding what hadn't yet transpired. Advice to Jane: always have a good novel to read in bed, don't waste too much time on reality. Advice to Franklin (assuming the departed could communicate with one another): bury your anger in a hole and walk away. To Avery and Jack: try being the greatest slabs of men that men can be. To Julian: I miss you and I'm going to find you. Yes, she knew that wasn't advice.

2009. She had not really thrown away the picture of Jane holding Franklin's ashes. Instead, she had stuffed it deep in her bottom dresser drawer and it had felt like it was gone. So that every time she dug it out it was a resurrection. Jane's face and fleecy jacket. The ocean in whitecaps. The way she held the box so carefully.

Fifteen years earlier, Veronica and Franklin had remodeled the kitchen (which they'd done once before, much more cheaply, when Jane was a child), and the same thing happened. A time capsule opened. The old wallpaper came off and the cupboards were removed and there, suddenly, was their daughter's nine-year-old handwriting. *Jane was here Nov. 7, 1972. I'm all out of air.*

The past's demands on the present. Look at me, indulge me for a moment before you slide the drawer shut, cover me up. Isn't it true that I'm all you have?

To which the rational mind answered, to which Veronica said, no. But. Remembering the young man from Grinnell. Telling herself they were naïve and new-bloomed and necessarily hopeful. That it wasn't what it was. Wasn't real. It affected her life with Franklin only in that his experience of her became his experience of her longing. Which changed, moved away from the young man and what could have been, roved, searched for a target, found him again, not him but a much older version of himself, whiskered, brittle, free. Longing enough to keep her alive. To undo her own dust. Veronica at rest not Veronica at all.

Examination

Anna passes her parents' bedroom and sees through the cracked door her mother standing in her underwear in front of a full-length mirror. Her mother raises her arms over her head and releases a blue bundle that tumbles down her body and becomes a dress. She adjusts its fit across her hips, zips its back zipper with a quick contortion and bunching up of material at the neck. She purses her lips to apply lipstick. It seems her mother's not really looking at herself, but at the pieces of herself she's assembling. The light in the room is slow, museum-like. "Morning, Anna," her mother says. Anna jumps.

In the kitchen, she puts two frozen waffles in the toaster oven. Her father is leaning against the counter, struggling to knot his tie. He gestures helplessly at himself. "Can you?"

The tie is the same deep blue as her mother's dress. She takes the slippery ends in her hands and pictures a proper knot, then undoes the image in her head, this loop, that tuck, and works her way forward to meet the undoing. She tugs at the crisp little knot.

"Thanks," her father says, and Anna's about to ask why he and her mother are getting all dressed up but stops herself. The toaster dings. She pours syrup over her waffles, feeling a stealth pleasure in having to supply the answer herself. Perhaps they're on their way to meet a child they gave up for adoption long ago. Perhaps that child's name is Emerald and she's written a book about her abandonment. And in the book, there are pictures of Anna's mother holding the little baby like a bag of apples. Anna knows that to come right out and ask might cause a) quarreling, or b) the proffered answer to be far less interesting than she'd hoped, less interesting than the alternative she's created.

Her mother pops her head into the kitchen and asks if Anna can buy her lunch today, and withdraws before Anna can answer. Her father lines up two coffee cups on the counter, fills them, and drinks them both. When her mother returns she smells like crushed roses.

"We're off," her mother says. "Don't forget to brush your teeth."

Her father calls over his shoulder, "Have a good day at school, my sweet."

Anna is waiting to hear something beautiful over the loudspeaker, something that makes beautiful sense. There are announcements, the clearing of a secretary's throat.

Today, her class is studying Other Cultures. Their teacher stands up front, modeling a kimono. "Mrs. Sharkey, what countries border Japan?" a boy named Gregory asks. "What are its influences?"

Mrs. Sharkey completes a revolution. "That's an excellent question," she says. "And the answer is China. And, I believe, Bangkok."

Anna can't help herself. "Japan is an island!" she calls.

She arrived at her sixth-grade classroom wearing plastic-framed, purely cosmetic spectacles. No lenses. When her class was taken to the infirmary for their back-to-school check ups, Anna was pronounced legally blind in one eye and given a prescription for real glasses. The nurse said *legally blind* in an exultant voice, as if she had been transported onto the set of a television show. She thumped her pointer against the eye chart, and her white cap, a corpulent dove, slipped to the side of her head. In seventh grade, Anna attempted to block a school-wide balloon-release project on ecological grounds, but the principal, who hoped that one of the balloons—with its cheery, rudimentary note—would reach the rich side of Alexandria, made her sit in a room with the spent helium tank and write extra notes for the kids who were absent. *I am a seventh-grader who loves Google Earth. It helps me with geography. I go to Hoover Intermediate. Our classrooms need new computers.* (To which the principal added *Preferably Macs.*) And now, in eighth grade, Anna is still waiting for her school, a crumbling brick building with a series of slender and mysterious chimneys, to be transformed into a temple of learning.

A guidance counselor knocks on Anna's classroom's half-open door and lets herself in. Although she knows perfectly well who Anna is, the guidance counselor, M. Clump, pretends to look up and down the rows for her. M. Clump wears a nylon pants suit and an engagement ring that has not been made good on. It is said, by students who have been disciplined in her office, that she makes weekly calls to the Pacific Northwest. Does she dream of that place, sky gray as a trashcan lid?

The teacher turns to M. Clump. She's used to being corrected by Anna, but she doesn't like it. "She's over there. Keep her as long as you need."

"Have you used the restroom?" M. Clump asks Anna.

Anna ignores the question.

"Where is she going?" Gregory asks.

"She's going to take a test," M. Clump says. "We're trying to get to the bottom of Anna. Anna is a bit of a mystery."

When Anna arrives at school each morning, she sees M. Clump sitting on the back stoop, where the cafeteria workers ferry buckets of government hamburger from delivery truck to refrigerator. There, M. Clump takes rapid sips from a coffee cup and closes her eyes for what seems to Anna the length of time necessary to have an unpleasant realization. The smell of thawing fish sticks, the pebbly breading coming unstuck, is overpowering at that hour, cast into the air by the kitchen's ventilation system. Birds rush past M. Clump's shoulders as if they are rounding the bend in a particularly grueling race.

"Have you used the facilities?" she asks more loudly, and again Anna ignores her. She follows her out of the room and down the long hallway. It is exhilarating to be out of class. Anna gives a little hop and skip. She thinks that she is the first student to feel such release, to walk briskly from the charted day into the unknown. There is an anarchic quietness to the place, a thwarted aggression in the bland bulletin board displays and the main office's bank of steel desks. They pass the library, from which a net of whispers emerges. The hallway slopes upward and the front doors of the school become visible. Two patches of light drop through the windows and stick to the floor.

"I want you to know that we're all very proud of you," M. Clump says as she guides Anna into her office. A clown-shaped popcorn machine stands in the corner. The popcorn is popped in the clown's throat and dispensed from its mouth. There are striped bags with crimped edges stacked next to it. M. Clump gestures to a chair. "I want you to hear me praising you and supporting you."

"I don't really know what I've done," Anna says.

"You've reached the moment when your life will go one of two ways," M. Clump says. "It's all just destiny from here."

Anna thinks that, while others dismiss the guidance counselor's powers of perception, she is in fact tragically aware.

"A man is going to ask you some questions," M. Clump continues. "You should just answer them without necessarily worrying about whether you're right."

Anna arranges three sharpened pencils in front of her. She has never been able to answer a question without worrying about whether she's right, or deliberately deciding to be wrong. She's loyal to the idea of clean ends and proper directions, As or Bs, yeses or nos. Recently her mother sat her down to have a talk about menstruation, and Anna was filled with dread at the thought of it—the blood, of course, and even the word *tampon,* which sounded to her like a piece of athletic equipment—of anything that threatened to split her life into before and after, of anything so broad.

She has brown hair that clings to her neck, long shiny legs, a heart-shaped mole on her ear. A girl of her age is bodily smooth, perfectly aligned, a figure of original, not reconstituted, beauty. Anna knows she will be pretty, because her mother is, though she's also starting not to be. A kind of sinking is setting in.

The office door opens, and a man wearing a white linen suit and jogging shoes walks in. "Hello, Anna," he says. "I've heard so much about you."

"Like what?" He's not intimidating. His bowtie is askew.

"Like, you stump the teachers." He raises his eyebrows at M. Clump. "My name is Edward. And I'm going to try to stump *you.*"

He shakes Anna's hand and tells M. Clump that her services are no longer needed. M. Clump lingers, scooping her hair into a dolphin-shaped clip. She opens the door to an adjoining office. "Do us right, honey," she says as she leaves.

Edward hangs his suit jacket next to the popcorn machine. "That was?"

"The guidance counselor."

"With the unemployment rate so high right now, she has a job?"

Anna shrugs her shoulders uneasily.

"Never mind," Edward says. "Let's begin." He sits down, using a second chair for a footstool, looks up at the ceiling, and narrows his eyes as if free-associating. "If I knew, somehow, that you would like popcorn, what would that be called?"

"Intuition," she answers. "A good guess."

"True or false. If some Smaugs are Thors and some Thors are Thrains, then some Smaugs are definitely Thrains."

"False."

"Which one of the five choices makes the best comparison? LIVE is to EVIL as 5232 is to: A. 2523 B. 3252 C. 2325 D. 3225."

"2325."

"If you rearrange the letters 'MANGERY,' you would have the name of: A. Ocean B. Country C. State D. City."

"City. No, country!"

Edward shakes his head. "Slow down, slow down. Why don't you tell me something about yourself."

Anna is annoyed. If he continues in this vein, nothing will be accomplished and she will have missed lunch. She'll be sent back to her classroom hungry. Mrs. Sharkey will look at her with a mixture of scorn and pity, and give her a package of crackers from her desk. She'll tell Anna to eat quickly and then silently participate in the remainder of the class's discussion, by listening. The Japanese, the teacher will say, are a graceful and increasingly commercial people . . .

"I *would* like some popcorn," Anna says.

"I suppose we can help ourselves."

Edward fills two bags. She watches disappointedly as the popcorn comes trickling, not blowing, from the clown's mouth. These things are always compromised by the roles they're asked to play. Birthday party cakes suffer from the same surfeit of expectation—all that green icing, the white hash marks, the frozen menace of the tiny plastic soccer players.

Edward says, "I'll start. I've already told you my name. I grew up on a farm near Lynchburg. I'm interested in child intelligence. If you pass this test, you get to go to a special school where you'll be among your peers, a magnet program for gifted children in D.C." He waits for some reaction from her, and adds, "Don't worry, you're not in trouble. You're in the opposite of trouble."

Anna eats a handful of popcorn. Edward gazes out the window at the flag tossed aimlessly about the flagpole. "Nice flag," he says, although it is frayed and faded.

"I saw a hallway monitor strap a kid to that pole with his belt."

It was June. Anna was seven or eight, in thrall with the appearance of things. She was eating some candy that her teacher had given to her. They were on a field trip. Everything was an explosion.

"We need to get back on track," Edward says. "What would be the result if planet Earth moved closer to the sun and equatorial countries became too hot for human habitation? A. Everyone flees North. B. Manufacturers of heat shields are inundated with orders. C. Vacations in cold countries become desirable. D. Panic."

"Panic," she says. "Panic."

"Good. Now what do you see when I show you this?" He raises a white placard with a baroque black mess of smears and blobs on it. It has no significance; it is the opposite of significance. Anna hates it.

"I see a lake with some canoes on it."

"And this?" He raises another, similarly chaotic placard.

"Ice-cream truck. No. Pinball machine."

"Which is it?"

"Either, really."

"My analysis of your answers depends upon their being one thing," he says.

"But I see more than one thing. I see like twenty things."

"You've got to winnow them down."

Anna watches the way light slices into Edward's hair, illuminates the separateness of its strands. "Edward," she asks, "did you go to a special school when you were my age?"

He begins to speak and she can tell from his expression and the way he's gesturing that he did not, that for one reason or another something stood in his way. He used to think he had a big future, a noisy one. She's imagined that kind of life for herself, too, events bubbling upward, pushing against the rim of the day.

"May I use the restroom?" she says.

He stops talking and nods. His neck is red.

At the sinks, she wipes her face with a wet paper towel that smells like dog food. A stall opens and a girl named Candace comes out. Candace is a distant descendent of Buffalo Bill Cody, whose likeness is plastered all over her locker. She has a tough and indisputable charm.

"No hall pass?" she asks.

"I've just come from next door."

"From Clump? Are you in trouble?"

Anna hesitates. "I'm being tested," she says.

"For what?"

"This guy shows me pictures that aren't pictures yet, and asks what I see."

Candace snorts and pumps soap on her hands. "Tell him you don't want him getting off on your daydreams."

Anna's stomach drops with new intent. She does not go back to the office where Edward waits. Instead, she walks quickly to the school's front doors and pushes them open. She walks past the flagpole, turning to wave to Edward in case he's watching. She crosses the basketball court and reaches the street. She waves to an old man mowing his lawn. Grass clippings line the edge of the sidewalk, glowing a deep green that seems to be released by the mower's blades. The old man's skin is . . . well, it frightens her. It is as if he is draped in his own disguise. He turns around and pushes his mower up the middle of the sidewalk, its engine still running.

She walks very quickly. Each house that is not her own spurs her on with its strangeness. She decides that if someone asks her where she's going, she'll shove him. It would be a him. The air is blue and the sky is thin. Finally, she comes to her front door, unlocks it, and goes inside. As she moves through the living room to the kitchen, she notes the place where the wooden floor stops and the linoleum begins. The clay donkey with the baskets of flowers strapped over its back. The platter of bananas and apples. She is rarely home alone, and when she is, objects take on a weight that she is blind to when her parents—the objects' keepers—are around. She unwraps a square piece of cheese and takes a neat bite from each of its sides. Her memory is not so distinguished as her ability to return to certain moments again and again. She remembers sitting in a pile of laundry in a clothes basket, staring out through the plastic grid. Once, she mistook a woman in the airport for her grandmother, and clung to the woman's woolen pants leg until she was removed. She felt, then, that the old lady had played a trick on her, singled her out and offered her the long, easily disguised leg.

Anna hears two pairs of shoes, two coats taken off and thrown over the banister. Her parents' voices jangle like separate recordings of the same song.

". . . wouldn't have liked that angel bit in the least," her father is saying. "Or the gold flutes on the programs."

"He would've hated it," her mother says. There is a pause. Anna knows her parents are looking at each other with that neutral gaze that signifies total complicity.

"I guess he doesn't care now," her father says.

"It's we who care," her mother replies. "Damn us."

When she comes into the living room, they are sitting together on the couch. Her mother's arm is draped over her father's shoulders. Her father's glasses are folded into his shirt pocket. Her parents register no surprise that she is home. Maybe they have lost track of time. That it was a funeral they'd dressed up for that morning—that they didn't tell her to protect her—makes her feel deeply ashamed.

"If you'll excuse me," her father says. Anna hears him walking down the hallway and then the scrape of a chair in his study. Her mother tucks a strand of hair behind her ear and feels her forehead, an automatic gesture. Anna waits for what seems the proper amount of time, then knocks on her father's door. He is sitting at a round table lit by a lamp with a tufted green shade. His gaze is distracted, inward looking, like a knot in a rope.

"What are you doing?" she asks.

"I'm writing a letter of condolence."

"What does it say?" And then, "Can it be from me too?"

"Why you?"

She sits on his lap and rests her face against his chest. "I want to be part of it." His chest is warm, his tie still perfectly knotted.

"Oh, Anna," her father says. "You are."

At dinner, the sound of silverware fills the room. She chews, swallows, takes sips of milk. The flame-shaped bulbs of the chandelier flicker but do not go out. She longs for the fluorescents of school, where everything appears equally on everyone's faces. "So, who died?" she asks finally.

"Do you remember—" her mother begins, at the exact same time her father says, "She wouldn't remember—"

She stirs her fork around on her plate. Its scrape is delicious.

"Someone you met once when you were very little," her mother continues. "A man who put me through college."

"Why did he do that?" Anna asks.

"Your mother was very talented," her father says.

"Don't listen to him," her mother says. "My family didn't have the money to pay for my education, and he did me a huge favor."

"Then why is *dad* sad?"

"He's sad for me," her mother says.

Anna thinks this is the beautiful statement she's been waiting for. It lisps like a bell in the back of her head. "Someone came to school today," she says.

Her parents' forks pause on the way to their mouths.

"A man. He . . . gave a speech."

"What kind of speech?" her father asks.

"About traffic safety."

Her mother laughs. "A look-both-ways-before-crossing speech?"

"I know." Anna's heart pounds. "As if we're kindergarteners!"

Her father smiles, and she sees the sadness leave his face and something kind and plain, something ordinarily happy, take its place. It's obvious he's remembering her then, and there will be a time, she knows, when she'll remember him too. Right now he's of the moment, he's everywhere. But when she's grown, when she's old, all she'll have is memory, changeable visions, changeable shapes.

And how might she remember this day? As her last, best opportunity to escape? Or the time she knew what she wanted, the time she left the traitorous inquiries of Edward behind and came home to where she was meant to be?

Or something in-between that, the place she usually resides. A place of torn loyalties, confusion of being. A place that leaves so much to be desired her imagination's had to grow too big, its roof wrenched off, its doors flung wide, everything open for inspection.

Sink Home

The first time Mira sees Hugh, he is trying to thread his body through an unstrung tennis racket. She's on one side of a crowded room and he's on the other, but there is a little gap in the crush of people and she watches him twisting his compact body sideways, hoisting up his pants leg, and stretching out a bare foot.

They're at a party hosted by a Brazilian named Flavio. Flavio is her husband's friend, but her husband is at home with the flu. This evening she has learned that there are certain people around whom she should be quiet because they will only agree with everything she says. Having been agreed with, she'll begin to make increasingly outrageous statements and to adopt a wry, scouring personality not at all her own, and they'll just stand there and let her. They'll let her defame herself, just as they'd let her strip naked if she started to. After an hour of this, Mira decides to be very demure with the next person she meets.

Who turns out to be Hugh. Who is struggling, failing to thread his body through the racket. A few people hoot. She crosses the room and offers her arm as a prop for him to use while he puts his socks and shoes back on.

"Did someone dare you to do that?" she asks.

"What?" he says.

She takes a sip of beer and realizes that she's a little drunk, a realization that coincides with finding the proper person to be a little drunk around. Her cells, she decides, are like grains of rice, and the alcohol is the water in which they've been simmering, and now they are perfectly fluffed.

"Have you ever done that before?"

"Not successfully." He pauses in the midst of pulling on his canvas shoe. "Want to see me smoke a cigarette really elegantly with my toes?"

She shakes her head. Gilberto Gil is playing on the stereo. Mira loves how Brazilian Portuguese sounds, especially when sung. Listening to the music is like watching a box of chocolates melt. People begin dancing awkwardly, for most of them are white Virginians, but Flavio stations himself in the middle of the room and gyrates like a sprinkler feeding a small lawn.

They exchange names, and then Hugh pulls on her hand and keeps pulling until it can be called dancing. He has small damp hands, hands she would normally shake off.

When she arrives home later that night the house is dark, but she knows that her husband isn't asleep. Daniel can never sleep when he's sick. His wakefulness is a hard-bristled brush probing down a length of pipe for the stoppage, the matter. Probing for her. She tosses her coat over a chair and switches on the lamp that stands next to it. The lightbulb pops, a delicate, terminal sound. It's then she feels her resolve leave her. Her resolve to do what? Be the high-spirited, generously idiosyncratic person she'd been at the party? The furniture in the room, the insensate couch, the silent piano, knows she isn't like that. The pictures on the walls know too, having been hung by a woman who more closely resembles someone indecisive, often mournful. And hung again. And again. Never in quite the right place. Holes from the artworks' first and second hangings strafe the walls like machine gun scars. Ruining, almost ruining the effect of the third or fourth hanging, the grindingly-decided-upon final position.

In the bathroom, she tucks her hair behind her ears, revealing eyes that gleam like oil. She places two Advils in her mouth and bends to drink from the tap. The pills fall from the back of her tongue to the side of her mouth, a caustic flash. She gulps the water, straightens. Daniel calls out to her.

Today she is on her fifth excursion with Hugh. Not date, because he knows she's married. They are just friends, they have both said so. Mira's promised to invite him to dinner to meet her husband, but she keeps putting it off. Her husband's a surgery resident and is at the hospital all the time, so it's natural that she and Hugh do things alone. Today, a mild fall day, they've decided to go apple picking.

"I was in line at the grocery store and the man behind me was talking to himself," Mira says to Hugh as she settles herself in his blue car. "He was mumbling, mostly, but then I heard him say 'Other being. I don't like higher being, but I can accept other being.'"

"I can too," Hugh says. He drives quickly, a little recklessly.

"What can't you accept?" Mira asks. It bothers her a little, the way Hugh seems just fine with the limitations that her being married places on their relationship. She wants him to strain, rail against the events that led them to this place in their lives where they can't be together. But she suspects that he doesn't see it that way. Why should he? He was involved until June with an Irish woman whose picture Mira found on the passenger-side floorboard of his car. The woman was sitting on a couch with her legs propped on the armrest. Her skirt fell away from the side of her thigh to reveal the lace-ribbed band at the top of her stocking. "Tiny breasts," Hugh had said, nodding at the picture. "Like little rubber squeaky toys." Mira flinched and turned to look at him. He was accelerating the car through a light that had just turned red. She'd almost requested that he take her home right then, but she hadn't, and the comment floated between them like a spray of strong perfume that became, as it dissipated, less and less offensive. She imagined Hugh running his fingers over the Irish woman's breasts, over the smallness of them, paying extra attention.

Now Hugh says, "I can't accept injustice." He's not kidding. He works as a lawyer for the ACLU and embraces causes of all sorts. Today he's wearing a small red United Farm Workers pin on his jean jacket, its bird with outstretched wings like an upside-down temple, steps cut into stone.

They drive through the orchard gates and park in front of a barn where turnovers and cider and billowing chef's hats inscribed with "Wilson's Orchard" are for sale. They collect baskets and a map, and set out to find the Tremletts's Bitters and Pink Ladies which Hugh claims are far superior to store-bought varieties. The branches of the apple trees are slanted skyward, as if the trees had been turned upside down and shaken. Picking the fruit—rising on her toes, grasping an apple and twisting her hand round and round until it comes off—elates her with its simplicity. She becomes greedy, nearly filling her basket at one tree, and then, as she moves on, following Hugh's receding form, she realizes that there are still so many trees ahead. They stretch in neat knotty rows as far as she can see. She thinks, You could feed the world from here, mash up all these apples and make applesauce for all the world's babies, and runs ahead to share this insight with Hugh who, she knows, will correct her. She likes being corrected by him because he puts his arm around her when he does so. It's an excuse for him to touch her, to guide her out of the damp tangle of her ideas. But this time he just laughs and asks if she wants to see him climb.

She says yes. Hugh takes off his shoes (he seems to shed them whenever he can) and begins to scramble up a tree. His jacket stirring the leaves makes the weirdly amplified sound of a scratchy record. As Mira watches him she thinks how pleasing it is to be with a near-stranger. All of her faults just fall away in the presence of a relatively unknown male. Not faults so much as tiredness, coldness, some unyielding quality. With women she fares not as well—in fact, she has never had many female friends. She doesn't possess the vivacity for it, the love of talk, the eye roving and condemning and sharing what it snags. But a man with whom she is flirting—subtly, gently—elicits from her little bursts of whimsy and ego which are, she has to admit, perhaps more sustaining than they should be.

Hugh peers down from the treetop. His cropped hair and

feet that clutch as adroitly as his hands lend him a sly, simian appearance. "If I fell, could you resuscitate me?" he asks.

"Daniel could," she says.

"What's Dr. Daniel like?" He pelts a rotten apple at her.

She leaps sideways. "*Fight Club* was his favorite book until he met me. He's a good cook. He knows the secret to tofu is frying the shit out of it."

"Is he good in bed?"

Mira doesn't know how to respond to this question. She could say yes, and tug a bit of jealousy from Hugh like a thread from a shirt cuff. Or she could say no, and let him imagine that she lives in the midst of terrible inadequacy.

The truth is, sex with Daniel is rare. Good when it happens, but easy, oh-so-easy to let slide. She's usually been asleep for an hour or two before he gets home from the hospital. He brushes his teeth and then gets in bed and wants to talk about his cases. At that point, she has to pee, and as she sits on the toilet she thinks about walking back into the bedroom and removing her underwear, letting it drop straight down her legs, a move Daniel probably wouldn't even be able to see in the dark. But it'll empower her, won't it, open a rusty-hinged gate to some mild kind of wildness? Dark and loose and strewn and soft? Yes! Yes it will. And casting aside her tank top will do the same. The thin cloth leaving her skin, the air replacing it . . . Once they're naked, something outside of themselves will take over, something more forceful and bare.

That's the hope, anyway. Usually she just flushes the toilet and gets back into bed and listens to Daniel complain about his bullheaded patients and the dim, disinterested nurses. She slings her leg companionably over his and inhales his stringent hospital smell, something like roses crushed with aspirin. It seems ridiculous to have ever thought of doing anything else, especially anything that involves heavy panting, exertion. How quickly that scenario dissolves in her mind and their usual neutered posture takes hold—his breath buzzing against her head, the blankets bunched at their waists.

Bees poke at the decaying apples in the grass. "The question should be, am *I,*" she says to Hugh.

"Are you?" He starts down the tree, then turns and drops from what seems a great height. He lands on his feet, staggers, falls to his knees, falls face down in the pulpy grass with his arms flung straight out from his sides. Mira laughs and waits for him to get up. He lies still. She stoops next to him, rolls his slack body over, and examines his face. He lets the tip of his tongue, ribbed and shockingly pink, protrude from his mouth.

Mira places her lips on his and lets out a quick puff of air. "There." He snatches his tongue back just as she does so, but his lips stay open. She does it again. "And there."

He whispers, "More air."

She bends to him again. He puts his hand on the back of her neck. She pulls away and, casting about for something to do, bites into an apple.

Hugh sits up and rubs his ankles. "You should wait to eat that until you've washed it. Fungicides are nasty business. Dithane'll mess with your reproductive organs."

"Then water probably won't do much good, will it?" She takes another bite. Her face is hot.

"Water's all you've got."

They walk back to the barn, where their apples are weighed. Hugh pays for hers.

She phones him a few days later at her husband's urging. "Daniel wants to meet you. He's baked an apple pie. Can you come over?"

She is hoping he'll say no.

He arrives with a bag of shade-tree-grown coffee. They sit at the unwashed kitchen table surrounded by breadcrumbs and newspapers. Daniel bustles about getting plates and coffee cups from the cupboard, grinding the beans, cutting huge pieces of pie. He is still wearing scrubs and clogs, though he's had plenty of time to change. He feels like a warrior in those clothes, Mira knows this. They are his warrior-pajamas.

"So," he says heartily to Hugh. "What do you do and how do you do it?"

"I live. Simply."

"So others may blah blah blah," Mira says.

"You know," Hugh says, "if you really think about that slogan, 'Live simply so others may simply live,' it fails to be inspirational. Simply living isn't enough."

"You're right, it's stupid," Daniel says. "I don't like slogans of any sort, or bumper stickers, or signs."

"What do you mean you don't like signs?" Mira asks.

"I don't like those signs in restaurant bathrooms that say 'Employees must wash hands before returning to work.' Makes me pretty certain they *aren't* washing their hands. No one likes being told what to do."

"You've never seemed to mind it."

Daniel's face clouds. He sits down with them and begins to eat his pie with frenetic sawing motions of his fork. Hugh compliments him on it.

"It's all in the apples," he says. "You guys picked a good bunch."

Silence. The busy, lonely clattering of forks against plates, a sound that Mira associates with the dinners of stilted 1950s families, the fathers remote, the mothers apologetic, the children lost in their own small caves. Just to make conversation, she says something that she regrets immediately. "I wrote a song today."

"A song?" Hugh's eyebrows rise.

"A song!" Daniel is overenthusiastic.

"A song," Mira repeats stupidly. "Yeah. I don't know."

"I was wondering who plays that thing," Hugh says, gesturing to the piano which juts from the living room into the foyer.

Mira hasn't mentioned her songwriting to Hugh yet. She is currently unemployed (and has been for ten months), and it's a way to pass the time. When she's sitting at the piano words come to her easily, half-truths that need not be wholly true, images of, she hopes, a certain beguiling dark beauty. Her singing voice is average, more like talking than singing, but that doesn't matter because she never performs for anyone. The song in question is one she's been working on for quite some time; this morning she finished it with a triumphant last notation and a crashing of piano keys.

Mira sips her coffee. "I do."

"You'll never catch her at it, though," says Daniel.

Hugh shrugs. "It's good to have secrets. Secret talents."

"Or underused ones," Daniel says. "Like, I'm strangely good at darts."

"Oh yeah?" Hugh says. "Let's play sometime."

"Definitely." They grin at each other as if something complex has been simplified. She coughs.

"Well, will you let us hear your song?" Hugh asks.

No, she thinks so determinedly that she forgets to say it out loud. Hugh and Daniel wait for her to speak. She straightens in her chair. "I have something both of you want."

Daniel blushes. Hugh smiles and crosses his legs.

"That's not what I mean." She struggles past a growing frustration, a white feeling that threatens to eclipse what she's trying to say. She's not a doctor-in-training, not a lawyer, not pleased with herself, not confident, not full of verve and vigor, not on fire, not at peace. She's not sure of what she is, and this uncertainty feels to her like possibility, like space.

"Believe me, you're okay," Daniel says. He begins to clear the table. "I see a lot worse everyday."

Mira walks Hugh to the door. She doesn't know whether to hug him. Will not hugging him seem too deliberate? Daniel can see them from the kitchen. The water that was running stops. Mira won't let herself look over her shoulder. Hugh is facing the kitchen, but his expression doesn't change. "Thank you," he says.

Then he's gone. It's an hour later and Mira stands in the bathroom unclasping her bra. She lets it slide down her arms, then raises it to her nose. The twin pockets of black cotton are still warm, and smell vaguely nutty. She thinks that when Daniel is at the hospital, confronted by so much need, it must be a kind of reprieve. A reprieve from worries about, or even consciousness of, his own weakness. But he can't ignore her, and her eccentricities bother him. He's gone to bed early even though it's his only night off for the next few weeks. She begins to cry. In the mirror, her face is hideous.

Mira and Hugh sit at a hotel bar with a long window behind it. The window is eye-level with an adjacent swimming pool, and occasionally they can see someone paddle by. A preponderance of fat children are in the pool this evening. Bubbles cling to their round bodies, shiny and thoughtless as beach balls, and are released in long, effusive trails.

Mira sips her vodka and grapefruit juice. "I think people are most honest when they're underwater."

"Why is that?" Hugh asks.

"Because you have to keep your eyes closed. Navigate by instinct."

He nods toward the pool's occupants. "I kind of want to close *my* eyes."

"Fat children often become thin adults. The overly thin adults of tomorrow. That sounds like the name of some reality show, doesn't it?"

He scuffs the tips of his shoes against the bar and puts his hand on her leg. His eyes look like puddles, they look tired. "It's good to be with you."

"You too."

"My apartment got broken into last night. Who knows why, it's a hovel. But they tore it up, took my stereo, my computer."

"Jesus. You weren't at home?"

"No."

She grinds her spine against the back of her seat. Don't do it, she thinks even as she asks, "Where were you?"

A pause. Like a forgotten line in a play, the unacceptability of silence. The terrible tension of waiting for it, worse for the audience than for the actor.

"With a friend," Hugh says finally.

Mira finishes her drink. You aren't together, you have no claim, she thinks. But how real everything feels, how swiftly her senses have been rearranged by him. She knows that, on one level, it is only flattery. She rises to and returns it easily. But there is something else, momentum. It is as if she and Hugh are walking along a road with snow heaped on either side of it, and the road is narrowing, the snow encroaching, the passable section becoming thin as wire. They are holding hands, their hands are ungloved but not cold, now one of them is walking in front of the other but still their intimacy is extraordinary, the intimacy of soldiers, refugees, people moving inexorably in one direction, moving without thought, without will, inches between them, less . . . Oh stop, she tells herself, what melodrama, what bullshit.

"Do you want another?" Hugh asks, gesturing to her empty glass. She nods. He attracts the attention of the bartender. "Vodka and grapefruit juice."

"A Greyhound," the bartender says.

"Yes, but please don't call it that," Hugh says.

She touches his elbow, slippery under his shirt. "What did the police say?"

"Not much. They came to the apartment, swept up the shattered glass, did something with tape on the windowsill."

A boy somersaults in the water in front of them. His hands flip frantically at his sides and his mouth is pinched into a grimace. When he stands, Mira cannot see his head, but she can see his heaving belly. A flap of fat overhangs the front of his trunks. Suddenly, a goldfish plunks down next to him. And another, another. They are being dumped into the pool. They make little orange slashes where they hit the water, then rove rowdy and glinting. They seem not to know where to go—the way they bump into each other suggests panic, goldfish-panic.

The fat children whoop and splash. The boy ducks back down and catches a goldfish in his mouth, spits it out.

"Let's go somewhere else," Hugh suggests.

"Your apartment."

"You don't want to see it," he says.

She insists. It is worse than she expected, demolished. Hugh's mattress has been knifed in two, his silverware dumped into the toilet, his books thrown onto the floor and doused with what looks like salad dressing.

"This is vandalism," Mira says.

"It's work-related. I didn't want to scare you."

They kiss and lie down on the torn bed. He pulls her shirt over her head instead of unbuttoning it. She wants to take something off him too, and as she sits up to do so he pushes her back down and parts her knees with his body and falls into her quickly, almost thoughtlessly. She is stunned. She grasps at his undershirt and bares his stomach which is so shiny it seems to reflect her. They jerk against each other. At the time it's not embarrassing, but afterward, when it's no longer necessary, Mira thinks the jerking—its rapidity, its mechanical need—was a little embarrassing.

Hugh rolls off her. "That was a surprise."

"Really?" she says.

"I guess not."

"Well, it should have been."

"Why? Would that make it okay?" he asks.

She stands up, aware of the angle of herself she's presenting to him. Her pubic hair is colorless, like sand, but thick and maybe even visible from behind. She's dizzy. The room tilts, the empty window swings to the ceiling and adheres there like a black postage stamp.

"That's not what I mean," she says. "I mean, something like that can't be planned." She puts her clothes back on.

"You felt good," he says.

He comes to her and loops his arms around her neck, hanging against her like a naked charm. "Promise me this. You'll sing your song for me one day."

She doesn't feel like promising anything. "What song?" she says.

Now she has a secret. Her pleasure and guilt are preoccupying. She doesn't think Daniel suspects anything, yet he does seem to be paying her more attention than usual, as if trying to win her back. He asks if she wants to go on a trip.

It is Sunday morning. They're sitting on the couch with their bare feet on the coffee table. "We could go to Chincoteague," he says. "See the ponies swim from island to island with their heads barely above water. It's triumphant, I've heard."

"Let's just take a walk," she says.

Mira's happy and also a little bit annoyed. When she lies

in bed with Hugh, the mattress ticking released by the knifing creates a kind of speed bump down the middle. The walls of his apartment still bear spray-painted profanities, the letters like flaming hoops. She is conducting a love affair on the premises of a crime scene. It bothers her that he hasn't cleaned the place up. It is his affinity for oppressed people, downtrodden people, people whom life has treated harshly, she thinks, that makes him reluctant to part with evidence that he too has been treated this way. When she meets him at the Metro after he gets off work, she notices that his collars are often dirty, his shirt pockets torn. "How does it feel to be the lone bohemian in downtown Washington?" she asks, and he laughs at her.

But now she's going for a walk with her husband. They hold hands for less than a minute. It is not clear who releases whose. In a park, a bald man wearing two enormous hoop earrings and a woman in a kind of patchwork pinafore are trying to teach themselves how to walk on a tightrope. The tightrope is about a foot off the ground, strung between two trees. The woman hops onto it, wobbles, and begins her mincing journey across.

Daniel whistles at her, a sharp, goading note. The woman looks to her left. Her red hair is nested atop her head like a pinwheel fireworks display. Her arms flap up and down, and she falls.

Mira, laughing, asks, "What was that? That was unlike you."

"Was it? You don't know."

"Of course I do."

"Everyone's got other sides to them."

She doesn't reply.

"Let me be my other side."

She feels a surge of warmness toward this man she made the colossal mistake of marrying. The fact that he doesn't seem to share in this opinion (they haven't spoken of it) only solidifies her conviction. Knowledge that searing, that sad, touches us singularly, she thinks. It is something to endure alone. But Daniel has always been good to her—in fact, she suspects it is his goodness that prevents him from examining their relationship and finding it wanting. He would never criticize something they'd built together.

They walk into a neighborhood known as Breederville, so called for the residents' tendencies to leave the playthings of their many children strewn about. Small bikes and tricycles lie at exhausted angles on the patchy grass. Garage doors stand open to reveal miniature basketball hoops, toy lawnmowers, shovels. There is something *alive* about these houses, crackling and kinetic; yet they also appear hastily abandoned. Mira has not given much thought to parenthood, but when confronted with its trappings—a wagon with a cape and a clawed-apart sandwich in it, for instance—she feels fairly certain it's not for her. Though how can she say, exactly? Trappings are the chaotic edges of the thing itself, the messy outer layer. Inside, she knows, people find love, abiding satisfaction.

Daniel has four younger siblings, ranging in age from eleven to twenty-four. When they visit his family, Mira scrutinizes his mother. Is she tired? She always cooks big meals and then waves everyone into the den to watch TV while she cleans up. Mira used to offer to help her with the dishes, but then Daniel took her aside and said that his mother had asked him to tell her to stop. That it just made more work. The fact that his mother wouldn't say this to her directly could have been a sign of tiredness, Mira thinks. Or is she interpreting tact as docility, old-fashioned manners as having had one's will trampled? She is an only child. Families confuse her. A small miracle, that so many people at so many different stages of their lives can live together in one house. A miracle, or a suppression of everyone's happiness. Maybe it's a little of both.

She picks up her pace and Daniel does too. They make a right at the end of the street and walk through a small commercial district. A Mexican restaurant, an antiques store, a coffee shop with fiberglass clouds mounted on a façade of painted-blue bricks.

They go inside. The espresso machine hisses and the baristas bang their equipment theatrically as they dump the used grounds. They rattle their silver pitchers, jugs of milk crowd the counter. She orders a latte. The cashier questions her intently about its temperature, its caffeine-to-steamed-milk ratio. As she waits for it, she notices a flyer on the bulletin board advertising an open mic night. A piano with a row of succulents on its bench sits in the corner. The fact of her coffee being made with such specificity fills her with a sense of purpose. She will go to the coffee shop and play her music. Daniel works on Thursday evenings, so he'll never know.

She arranges to have Hugh pick her up. The open mic starts at 8:00. She sits in her living room and drinks wine out of a coffee cup, nostalgic for this home she's made and might just as easily abandon—the wine pooling blackly in the bottom of her mug, the candlesticks and small wooden birds on the mantel, all the inanimate things speaking forgivingly to her, staking their little claim. A buffet drawer has been left open—what would it feel like to yank it out, upend it? What terrible relief would it afford? But she does not do that. She puts on her coat and stands on the front stoop, peering down the street. A car pulls into her neighbor's driveway, its headlights discovering her stranded, unbecoming. She waves.

Men drive so they can be in control of comings and goings, she thinks. She's glad to generalize right now, for it keeps her from considering her situation too closely. From admitting that she *wanted* Hugh to drive because she likes the feeling of him shepherding her places, as if she's an arrangement of flowers that he's delivering. Driving her quickly in her color, her glory.

A few minutes later, she goes back inside and dials his number.

"You want to know where I am," he says by way of greeting.

"I do," Mira agrees.

"I fell asleep. I'll be right there."

His car is cold. They do not talk on the way to the coffee shop. After they've parked and gotten out, she notices that he's wearing sweatpants with bulky pockets. The fact that he's carrying around his wallet and maybe his cell phone in the pockets of his sweatpants depresses her more than his lateness. It seems so desperate, the way a vagrant would transport a cigarette lighter and a bottle of NyQuil. She smells incense on his hair.

"Blue tiger?" she asks. "Emerald tranquility?"

"Is what," he says.

"Never mind." They're standing under one of the fiberglass clouds. Suddenly, there's a loud crack. The cloud drops to one side, swings back and forth.

"Oops," Hugh says listlessly. He doesn't move.

Mira has jumped to the side. "Hugh!" The cloud is just waiting to plummet, it is earth-bound, it wants to sink home. "Get out of the way!"

"What if it's in *my* way?"

She finds the owner, a heavily bearded man who wears a T-shirt with an image of the Marx Brothers on it, and tells him what's happened. He's not apologetic. He acts, in fact, as if she may have had something to do with the precariously dangling cloud, which is starting to look more and more like a pile of mashed potatoes. Finally, he fetches a ladder and some nylon cord. Mira watches Hugh watch him climb the ladder and reposition the cloud and anchor it with the cord—those things are just tied there?—and she sees bald admiration on his face for this supercilious man, this shop owner who, he must imagine, turned his back on the world of ideas to nobly serve people. She goes inside and signs her name at the bottom of the list of open mic participants. A young woman sits on the makeshift stage with a washboard and some spoons and sings a song about frogs. The small audience claps politely. A man clutching a sheaf of papers takes her place.

The latitude of love the man says, closing his eyes and weaving his shoulders back and forth. He pauses. *Oh yeah.* More weaving. His neck is muscular and pinkly ridged, like a sphincter. Mira closes her eyes too.

Left me freezin'! he shouts. Her eyes fly open. What am I doing? she thinks.

Then she sees Hugh, who's standing in the doorway scanning the room for her. She waves to him. Exuberant now, he crosses to her and cups her face in his hands and kisses her. She wishes all kisses could be the same, but they're not. Some are the hot point around which everything else rotates. This one is greedy and slipshod.

"Well, you're getting your wish," she says.

"What wish?"

"To hear me sing."

"I have so many, but—it's weird—there's nothing I really need. I'm totally satisfied."

"You are?" she asks cautiously.

"Satisfied the way a person can be whose desires are everything to him, and nothing." He pauses. "You're one of them."

"Your desires?"

"That's everything and nothing." He laughs, a rasp. "Do you understand?"

"No," she says. Hugh moves to a table in the back of the room. The man has stopped reciting his poetry. It's her turn.

She rests her fingers on the piano keys, which have been quiet for a long time. Quiet until she came along with her vanity and vice, and the hope that if she touches them artfully enough they'll be artful in return. She begins playing. People continue to talk, the espresso machine continues to exhale its hot breath of steam. She sings. The words don't matter, something else matters. Her voice grows louder and more confident, and blood fans out through her chest and her legs and arms and comes back to clap against her heart. Then, although she would have liked to remain the object of the small pieces of attention that float about the room, she finishes. There's applause. She rises. Hugh comes forward as if he's going to congratulate her, catch her in a hug, but instead he passes her right by and sits at the piano.

The ease and lack of effort with which he plays is almost condescending. You should have told me, Mira thinks. *I'm telling you now,* the voice of the piano says. It rises and falls like a path in the woods, a bridge over an icy river, something that demands compliance.

She starts clapping much too soon.

Hugh stops playing and turns to her. "Will you shut up," he says. "I mean, I was just getting started." He pushes the piano bench back and walks out.

She waits for him to reappear, standing still at the side of the room. People glance at her, glance around, surmise that he's not coming back, and begin clearing their tables. The baristas polish the nozzles of the espresso machine with folded wet cloths, they untie their aprons. The owner carries the succulents back to the bench. "That guy was an asshole," he says.

"Let me help you." Her hands shaking, she divides a stray glass of water among the five plants. Or are there six? She counts them (five), and buttons her coat, and takes off her earrings, and places her earrings in her pocket.

Outside, the stars appear vehemently tossed. Car doors slam and engines start. A little time passes during which she gazes at the sky, and then nowhere in particular. The employees of the coffee shop emerge and bid each other goodnight in high bright voices, and then the owner locks the front doors and belches. He scratches his crotch, raises his fingers to his nose, tips back his head as if to allow himself the full effect, and inhales.

Mira starts toward home. The park is quiet this time of night, the benches empty. She approaches the house just as Daniel does, coming from the opposite direction. He always walks to and from the hospital.

"Mira!" He half-runs to meet her. "I'm so glad to see you. Because it was the strangest thing . . ."

Their windows are full of light. "Let's go inside," she says.

"No, I've got to tell you." He grips her wrists. "I had a patient tonight who looked just like you, only, don't take offense, more beautiful. Like a heightened, sleeping you."

She turns her wrists in his hands. He releases them and holds her by her fingertips.

"And when we worked on her, I was shaking. I should have excused myself but I didn't. I opened her up and I saw inside." He keeps talking, and Mira thinks that he experienced with this woman something he's never experienced with her, that even sleeping her deep, druggy sleep she must've seemed to embrace him. "I had such power over her," he says. "Every decision was mine to make." He lets go of her fingers. "I wanted to release her from her pain."

Mira starts toward the front door but still he stands there, stunned by his admission. She's cold. She's so cold! "Come on," she says, turning back to him. "Come inside. Release me from *my* pain."

"I don't know how to."

"Pretend you do," she says.

Salvo

Leah and Ian were hunting for garbage. Leah was getting bored. "Show a little skin!" she shouted at the men loading onto buses in the outdoor plaza of Tucson's Greyhound station. The men had wily, rash-red faces, and shuffled forward in jerks as if pursued by the jabbing handle of a rake. Heads turned in her direction. A man carrying a wooden dowel with a newspaper draped over it didn't look away. He mounted the bus steps backward. Leah imagined he thought he was staring down a wild animal.

Ian took a Polaroid of a condom package sitting in a square of dust on the dashboard of a car. It didn't have to be strictly garbage, odds and ends worked too, little hopeless dashes. When he went home and made a painting of this picture, he would use only the most flattering colors. He was incredibly respectful of the gauche ornaments of the world.

A woman came out of a tobacco store. "That's my little girl's Pulsar!" she called.

Ian straightened. "I'm just—"

"It doesn't matter. I'll sell it to you."

He stepped back from the curb waving the Polaroid in the air, then extended it to her. "Would you like this?"

"No." Her hair looked run through repeatedly by fingers. "I'll sell it to you for two hundred dollars. There's some good shit in that car if you know what I mean and where to look and how to let it hit you. Some people don't know how. Have to open yourself along your extremities."

They began to walk away. The woman called, "What'd I say?"

It wasn't what she'd said, it was the spots of need—like perfectly round Band-aids—where her eyes should have been. Leah felt close to Ian, moving down the sidewalk. He was wearing sandals whose soles were made from Goodyear tires, he was putting one salvaged sole in front of the other with that long, loose-hipped strut of his, and for once she was part of where he was going.

"Two hundred bucks," he mused. "Maybe I should have."

"But you're anti-car."

"But I'm pro-helping people."

"These things collide every day," Leah said. Her shoes were Mary Jane–style Doc Martens. Her ankles were barely buried bones. They walked back to Ian's apartment and leaned into the kitchen counter, gulping water. Ian drank a fantastic amount of water. His skin was extremely well-hydrated, a taut liquid cover that showed no damage from the sun. On the counter, there was a lidless plastic container filled with apple cores, squash and onion skins, Yerba mate leaves, the crouching white heart of a pepper. It stank. Ian claimed he couldn't smell anything. When he emptied it onto the larger compost heap outside, brown rivulets splattering down after the clumpy, partially decomposed stuff, Leah would ask him, "*Now* can you smell it?" and he would shade his eyes from the sun to look sadly at her. The question was wrong, the question was wasteful. Leah didn't want him to stop composting, she just wanted an acknowledgment of the underside of his golden sense of purpose.

They were to be married in a week.

They'd met at the funeral of a mutual friend who had been killed in a traffic accident. Ruben had been riding his motorcycle without a helmet. The accident occurred late at night, three or four a.m., later than was fun to be out, and he was speeding south toward home. He had been marching against a proposed dog track near Phoenix, and must have then joined some of the other marchers for drinks, because there was alcohol in his system.

But how did they know? Leah kept wondering. Can a person be dead *and* drunk? Can a body accommodate all that nothingness? She imagined the hands of paramedics raking over Ruben, lifting him, prodding him for sobriety and vital signs. Propping open one of his eyelids with his swept-feather lashes and shining a penlight into his eye.

She had never told him how much she liked him. At the funeral, she kept thinking, Now you've lost your chance. She was distraught for him, of course, but somewhere inside that was a pin-drop of sadness for herself. For what could have been, the indisputable promise of the unfulfilled. The absolute sway of it. There was a café in an old hotel in town with a rotating case of desserts: four-layer coconut cake, chilled coffee mugs packed with chocolate mousse. They could have dined there together, all the delights twirling for them, and after making their selection watched the waiter pause in front of the case until what they wanted came into view. Opening the door halted its rotation. It was a dance.

Actually, they had eaten there together. They'd shared a piece of blueberry pie, but it didn't count because they were only friends then . . .

She looked at the person sitting beside her, who happened to be Ian. His cheeks were wet but he was not, at that moment, crying. Mariachi played, trumpets like alarms. The music did not inject a sense of defiance before death's finality into the air. It seemed, rather, as if the wrong CD had been selected. Mourners filed past the closed coffin, placing offerings on top. There was a picture of a young Ruben standing next to a horse, his hand on the animal's blank flank; a package of candy made from prickly pear cactus; an empty wallet. An empty wallet! Leah's heart protested this. She'd brought a snow globe whose interior swarmed with tiny glow-in-the-dark fireflies. It was a sweet thing, and it seemed, suddenly, that it didn't want to be left. The fireflies bobbed beseechingly. Whether these tokens were to be buried with him she did not know. She put the snow globe back in her bag, and sort of caressed the end of the coffin as she walked by. It was like hugging a piano.

Ian was outside, standing on the steps. He was wearing black jeans, and the tip of his tie was flipped over his back. "How did you know Ruben?" she asked.

He swung around. "Art school. We both dropped out."

"Nice that you could do that together," she said.

"He was completely broke."

"And you?"

"I didn't need the infrastructure, I guess."

She sat down. People began leaving the church, their shoes crunching the crushed granite drive, a gold-panning sound, restless. There was an undisclosed and definite time, it seemed, when staying at the service any longer would be to have to witness the family in their undiluted grief, and no one wanted to do that. Twice, wingtips stabbed Leah's backside. She winced. Ian watched her for a minute and then said, "Get up."

"Everything around here's dust," she said.

He pulled at her arms. The more he tried to lift her the heavier she felt herself to be. Finally she was on her feet and the roofs of the cars in the parking lot, like raised shields, threw their light against her. "Not everything," he said.

She stood looking out at the brown landscape. She was being unfair. The desert sheltered wild bursts of color. A yellow blossom on a cactus was like a birthday present on a stake.

"You should call me," he said.

"I don't know your number."

"Ian Spinney. Look me up."

She called the next day, but no one answered. Later he told her that he'd just been sitting there, letting the phone ring. She called again in an hour, and this time he picked up and invited her over. She arrived at his apartment clutching a bottle of wine she'd selected for its raw-toned label. She was an editor at a vanity press, in possession of a minor beauty she did not know how to magnify, and there was Ian thrillingly paint-splotched opening the door for her. A woman would have showered if she was having someone over, Leah thought.

But a man could walk around like an advertisement for compulsion.

Sitting cross-legged on the floor, they drank the wine. Leah's stomach churned with grief and longing. Longing for the grief to be gone—it was a roulette wheel, a little local tornado. They did not talk about Ruben. She had planned to, but for some reason, at the very moment the words were tapping against the inside of her mouth, she decided to kiss Ian instead. She lunged toward him. He understood her purpose and met her gracefully halfway. They were on their knees, heads together, as if conferring over blueprints.

"I'm sorry," she said.

He squeezed her hands. "Don't apologize. That was great. Do you want something to eat?" She nodded and followed him into the kitchen. He rooted around in the refrigerator and emerged holding two carrots covered in a fine fur of carrot hair. "You can only be sad up to a certain point, and then the idea of sadness takes over," he said.

So they were going to talk about Ruben after all. "I haven't gotten there yet," Leah said.

"It's repetitive, mostly."

She took a big, gnashing bite. She knew right away that these untarnished things were what Ian lived on.

"I keep thinking of it in simple terms," he said. "Ruben's crossed a bridge over a river, taken off in an airplane that has no intention of landing."

"Passage."

"He was zipping along on his motorcycle. He probably thought he was still driving."

"But that's awful." She imagined Ruben's speedometer registering an unnatural number, and him not knowing, racing along, faster, faster, gripping his handlebars in all his confused dying. Like a child . . .

"Would you rather he knew what was happening?"

"Of course not. But the headlights, the rushing air."

"Details," Ian said.

"I felt something for him," she said.

He leaned toward her with a slanted smile, as if he were taking her into his confidence and not the other way around. "Of course you did."

The dress was long and straight, with a scooped neckline and capped sleeves. Wearing it, Leah felt as if she were about to be tucked into bed between very expensive sheets. She'd purchased it quickly after she and Ian had agreed to get married, the natural conclusion to a 'Why the hell not?' conversation. The dress had come with a veil, the idea of which Leah had resisted. She had actively resisted it, yet somehow the veil, a filmy little scrap, had won. It was medium-length, with a loose weave like the screen of a fly swatter. She certainly wasn't going to allow it to cover her face. Regarding herself in the bureau mirror, turning this way and that, she thought, Silly.

Silly but nice. Many things were like this. Holidays. Wallpaper. Physical affection. French braids.

Just then, Ian backed into her bedroom, carrying a cardboard box which he dropped onto her bed. She peered inside. Vials of gesso and dried sponges and paperbacks were all mixed together. A chopstick marked his place in Wendell Berry's *What*

Are People For? He was moving in with her, bringing his belongings one bike-load at a time.

"Am I not supposed to see you in that?" he asked.

"It doesn't matter," she said, shrugging.

"Because you look really beautiful."

"Then gaze away."

"Did you know the wedding veil predates the dress by centuries? Yellow in ancient Greece, red in Rome. It's a relic of the days when a groom would just, whoosh!, throw a blanket over the head of the woman he wanted and cart her off."

"How romantic," Leah said.

She took a step and almost tripped on the long skirt. "Walk it off, walk it off," Ian instructed, so she kept going, stumbling from her bedroom through the living room and to the screen door. The air smelled of a scent released by crushing.

"What are *you* going to wear?" she called to him.

"I need to figure that out." His voice was close, a murmur on her neck.

"I guess you would've had to rent a tuxedo long ago?"

"Or become the kind of person who rents tuxedos long ago."

"Well, do you think I'm really . . . this?" she asked, waving a hand at her dress.

"No. I don't." Ian unzipped her gently, and guided her to the couch.

"Yet."

He stripped too. "Be true to yourself above all else, Leah. Don't do anything that doesn't just roar out your name."

"You're naked."

"So?"

"You can't make an argument that way."

"Distract me, then," he said.

She looked at his empty shorts cupping his boxers, a lily pad and its bloom. She looked at his face and saw its expression change, a crumpling of self-regard. He was a generous lover.

"Okay," she said.

Once, Leah and Ruben drove out into the desert to go camping, to the shadows of the Rincon Mountains. They lay on their sides on sleeping bags, she facing him, he facing the wall of the tent. He was wearing only a pair of cut-off corduroys. She stared at the place where his hair touched his neck and wondered if she could disguise her fingers there.

"I'm hot," he said.

"Me too." She fiddled with the zipper on the tent's flap. "There's no breeze."

"Will you take my shorts off?"

She laughed.

"No, really." He had a talent for making these requests sound perfectly normal. In this way, he recruited allies and admirers, people who wanted to be in on the spontaneity. "I'm so hot I can't move."

"I'm not your mom, Ruben," she said even as he rolled onto his back, spreading his arms in a gesture of helplessness. She paused. His nipples were like the knobs of a simple wooden puzzle. "Oh, for god's sake."

"You have to unbutton them," he said, as she tugged at his waistband. He continued to gaze up at her. "Fie."

They had been trying to think of words whose meanings were represented perfectly by the way they sounded.

"Doesn't really sound like anything. Chanteuse."

"Nice one. Floater."

"What's that?" she asked.

"A corpse found in a body of water," he said.

"Too irreverent."

"Well, there's something irreverent about dead people."

"You're just saying that because you want me to accept floater. Which I won't."

"But picture it," Ruben said, "the gases, the sprawled limbs, dying on, like, the toilet, maybe a tiny silver toilet on a train. Or this. An obese woman on a roller coaster. You know how it's going to end."

"Lift your hips," she said. He did so, and she slipped his shorts off. "What a cheap thrill, huh?"

"A thrill."

She lay down next to him and took his hand. This was something they did every now and then.

"Barnstorm," he said.

The ceiling of the tent was being trammeled by insects. They made a flurrying, ticking sound. A blizzard. She dropped Ruben's hand and went outside, skirting a cluster of Cholla cactus like elongated, spiky grapes. It was nearly dark. The tent was a small pitched church. She sat down. Ruben crawled to her and began to rub her back. Leah closed her eyes, resting her head on her arms. The book she was editing, *You Can't Spell Slaughter Without Laughter,* about the genuine happiness the author experienced working in a meatpacking plant, was proving difficult. "I am still alive, me, me," the author wrote after describing all the swinging carcasses. That he was at considerable advantage over a corralled animal didn't seem to occur to him. The only satisfaction she'd gotten was in scribbling *Preposterous—please verify* in the margins, or deleting large chunks of text, but even so it was more like hiding something than banishing it for good.

"There, there," he said, "wife o' mine."

"What?" she asked.

"I'm pretending you're my wife, and I'm soothing you, though I don't understand what you're upset about to begin with." He was stroking her roughly. "I'm practicing."

"You don't need to."

Ruben wore his hair in a buzz cut, which highlighted the strict bones of his face. His skin was brown and copper and gold. "Why not?"

"For men, nothing really changes," Leah said.

"You're being cynical. You think it's cute."

"I'm never getting married."

"No, you don't seem the type."

"Why is that?" she asked.

"You're at your best when you're a little lonely, Leah."

She did not think that was true. She liked other people, their exclamations and opinions, though she often didn't agree with them. Was that loneliness, standing in opposition to others? "I'm going to sleep in the car."

"Okay," he said, shrugging.

The breadth of his shoulders and the slightness of the gesture combined to make Leah feel stung, spurned, dizzy. She walked a few steps away, then stopped and looked back. He'd disappeared into the tent.

"Besotted," she said.

Ian finished moving his paintings to her place. There was one of a child's crown, gluey blots where jewels had gone, dangling from the raised flag of a mailbox. Another of a doghouse wholly occupied by brown weeds, overturned dish at its door like evidence of a last battle. The condom from the other day—she just happened to spot it—was done beautifully, the square package, like the skin of an orange, appearing to contain something crisp and nutritive. It practically bulged with promise, and there, mostly visible, was the phrase *Ultra Pleas*——.

She sat down. These pieces asked for some amount of interpretation, but how much? Ian, who was stacking them against the living room walls ten, twelve deep, was frustratingly silent about his work. Leah suspected it was part of some philosophy—maybe the trash and riff-raff were supposed to speak for themselves. Maybe they were supposed to take on an ineffable second life.

She said something she hadn't intended to. "It's funny we never met before Ruben's funeral. I remember how you cried there."

"What are you talking about?" he asked.

"I was sitting next to you, and I saw tears on your cheeks."

"I didn't cry at Ruben's funeral," Ian said. "I expressed my sadness by shacking up with his woman. Made me feel close to him."

"I wasn't his woman," Leah said.

She turned again in her memory to the funeral. Actually, she had seen the after-effects of tears, not the tears themselves. They proved nothing and hinted at too much, they were benignly controlling.

"You sort of theoretically were," Ian said. "He talked about you."

"He did?"

"I think. I remember him saying someone was intense. That was you, right? I mean," he added quickly, seeing her face, "it was a compliment, coming from him."

Leah knew he didn't mean her any harm. She went into the bathroom to change for the pre-wedding party that their friend Dennis was having for them. There were two toothbrushes in the holder now. The bristles on Ian's were made from boar hair.

They rode their bikes to Dennis's. Occasionally one of them would shift gears, or swerve to avoid broken glass. It was that time of evening when the birds were most rapacious about the little dates in the palms. Mountains ringed the city. The sun was setting and everything, everyone looked gauzy and grateful, skating through light.

At the party, the other women surrounded her, congratulating her and touching her shoulders. "You've forgotten Ruben so soon?" someone named Nancy asked.

"Of course I haven't," she said.

"Then what's all this?" Nancy gestured at the artichokes and Capiz dishes filled with butter, the Mexican candles, the bottles of wine and beer.

"This," Leah said, "is one thing. Ruben was another."

"You were always together," Nancy said. The other women nodded their heads. "We were all waiting for something to happen, not that we had a particular stake in your happiness or anything. We waited and waited. It spawned a drinking game. Like, drink if Leah or Ruben repeats something that the other has already said. Or, drink if Leah or Ruben bails on a party shortly after the other does."

She was shocked that their friendship had been on such display. She'd always thought it private, rather select. "Sounds fun."

"Oh, it was, in a boring way," Nancy replied.

Leah returned to Ian, who was being advised by Dennis and his girlfriend Mary about where they should go on their honeymoon. They hadn't decided yet. The idea was they were simply going to jump in the car and drive and see where they ended up.

"North," said Mary, "you'll run right into that tried and true vacation spot."

"The Grand Canyon?" Ian asked.

"No, Canada," Dennis said, and everyone except Leah laughed.

"Why not Canada?" she asked.

"We're not going there," Ian said. "Not on our first trip together, at least."

"Not on your first trip," Mary echoed, her face devout with agreement.

Leah rocked backwards and Dennis steadied her. "But I want to," she said. "British Columbia, Vancouver, the coast and mountains. Cleaner, colder. Kinder, maybe."

Mary was wearing a T-shirt that said *The Weather Is Here—Wish You Were Beautiful.* She wandered toward the serving table, and Ian followed her.

"How did we find each other?" Dennis whispered.

"It's one of those mysteries," Leah said.

They watched Mary make quotation marks in the air. "Not a mystery, an accident," he said.

Why was this so reassuring? When other people admitted to mistakes, why did it make her feel so entrenched, so safe?

"A happy accident?" she asked.

Dennis nodded almost indiscernibly. "Sometimes."

She went out to the patio, where Nancy was sitting in a canvas chair. The moon was the color of the rocks in the rock garden, and the rocks in the rock garden the color of Nancy's long pronged fingers, which clamped a cigarette and moved it to her mouth unhurriedly. "Don't talk about him," Leah said.

Nancy exhaled. "What's gone is gone forever, but memory just won't fucking leave. Does that seem fair?"

Smoke scratched against her face. "Yes."

The last time she saw Ruben, she dallied about reading to him from the newspaper. They were sitting in his bedroom. She didn't know it was the last time. "Her habit of wiping down plastic surfaces on planes and in hotels was all about control," she read aloud.

"Oh, that Ashley Judd," Ruben said.

She raised her eyebrows.

"I mean, I'd do her."

"That's valiant."

"No. You think"—his finger waggled between them—"this is all I need. But I have appetites!"

She looked back down at Ms. Judd's elfin face. So tragic, she thought, your plastic surfaces. Her own neuroses were mostly unexplored, but she had great faith they were more noble than that. Maybe it was the exploration that did them in. Better that they just sit there and portend.

"Am I pretty?" she asked.

"Of course you are."

"No, I'm not. Not really."

"Why do women always say that?" he moaned. "It's the most clumsy lack of confidence."

His cat writhed about their legs. The cat would urinate but not defecate in a litter box, and left dry, caterpillar-shaped pellets all over Ruben's apartment. Just then, it stooped next to Leah, rippling from its mottled little neck to its whip-like tail.

"She feels comfortable around you," Ruben said.

"Who won't she shit around?" she said.

"I have one friend who makes her completely constipated."

She wondered, ashamed, if perhaps the cat's condition arose from what it witnessed this friend and Ruben doing. "Have I met her?" Leah asked sharply.

"No, you haven't met *him,*" Ruben said, "but your jealousy is touching."

"I know. That's why I do it."

"I thought maybe there was more to it than that." He stood up. "Be right back."

Leah sat very still. She didn't even want his body—she wanted what was behind it, inside it, the dark place called

Ruben. To be someone else. To be someone else's someone else. Padded by their memories, protected by the most basic fact of their being. He returned with a wad of paper towels and a bottle of Citrusolv. As he removed the cat's mess, he told a scatological joke. "Ruben?" she asked.

"Yeah?"

"So who are your 'appetites' for?"

"Strangers, mostly," he said.

Leah and Ian were married by Dennis, who'd become ordained as a Universal Life minister to do so. People clapped when they kissed. Leah hadn't expected this. She looked up shyly, her veil peeking out from behind her ears, and the guests thought, Oh, that would have been a nice picture. So rarely is Leah's face unconstrained by knowledge of itself! There was a reception afterward and then a night at the Arizona Inn, where they touched each other in a self-congratulatory way, as if they were touching themselves.

The next morning, they left on their road trip. Ian was wearing a sweatband that made a stiff ruff of his hair. He sat with a pitcher of sun tea wedged between his feet. Leah drove. They had not discussed their destination since the night at Dennis's, but she steered north onto the highway that would take them to Phoenix, up into Utah, Idaho, Canada maybe. She wasn't sure they were going to Canada, but they were going toward it. The car was a dart, equal parts hope and aim.

Ian kissed her neck. "I have almost no memory of the actual ceremony," he said. "Did Dennis go into the ''til death' part?"

"I wasn't really listening either," she admitted.

"You weren't listening?"

"Isn't that what you just said?

"I meant I was listening too well."

She felt a swell of tenderness for him, for the way he'd never be exactly who she wanted and she would always walk around with a nest of dissatisfaction and guilt and, strangely, the desire to protect the person she felt this about. It would be a tangled thing, made of fibers plucked here and there, from the recesses of herself and the sunny exposures of him, from her carelessness and his care, from her shoes toppled in the closet on his sandals.

She let out a breath. "Whatever he said, it worked."

"True," Ian said.

They were nearing the site of the accident. She happened to look over at the other side of the highway, happened to or needed to or knew to—something caught her attention, diverted her for a split second—and that's when she saw it. A white cross, a little protrusion from the dirt. She wrenched the wheel of the car to the left and they crossed the dividing strip. Ian said something, but she ignored it. He said something else but she pulled over, got out of the car leaving the keys in the ignition, and walked just a few steps to crouch in front of it.

It was dishonest. As if Ruben had simply pointed his motorcycle in this direction and *puff!*—when the smoke dissipated two strips of wood were nailed together in his place. She had never suspected something like this would be erected for him, but she hadn't known his family very well. Then she noticed a tiny helmet, throwing off light, had been painted right where the two pieces of wood met.

Ian was coming toward her. "You did this," she said.

"It was a gesture."

"You decorated it."

"It can be from both of us."

No it can't, Leah thought. The helmet was red with a white chin strap and the waves of light squiggly, cartoon-ish, and Ruben would never have worn such a thing. He thought the future happened when the present wasn't strong enough, he thought the people of the present were kings. She kicked at the cross and it came easily apart. She kicked at it again. Ian stood watching her. When he bent to the pieces and picked them up, she thought he meant to take them with him to paint them, later, and she felt rage replace her petulance. But he turned and threw them in high, choppy arcs out over the desert scrub, flipping, giddy, a little explosion of the actual into a better shape.

Celebrants

We cornered April in the living room. She'd just left Adam. "Why now?" Margo asked. Her glasses, perfectly round, and her expression—as if she were searching perpetually for something wily and distant—lent her the appearance of a person peering through binoculars. "Why ever? You and Adam seem destined for great things."

April smiled and said, "Seemed."

"This is serious," I said. "Your life is serious."

She ignored me. "To answer your question, dear M., I've come to hate certain gestures of his, elemental things. The way he swallows, for instance. The way he breathes."

"You broke up with Adam because you don't like the way he breathes?" I asked. It sounded perfectly reasonable, actually—it was the timing that I objected to.

Adam belonged to a club called the Re-enactors, about which I felt a great deal of scorn and curiosity. The club had many ceremonies, the better to intrigue people like me. One of these ceremonies, due to take place in a week, was an official welcoming of members' girlfriends into the inner sanctums. April had already received her invitation.

"Oh phooey," Margo said, as April walked away. We could hear her footfalls on the stairs. "She was going to memorize every detail of the ceremony according to mnemonic devices. Who was there, the timbre of the music, the oaths of fealty. I get dizzy just thinking of it going on without her."

I began to pace around. There was something dense and appealing about Margo, like a good wet piece of clay. "I can bear my own disappointment, but I can't bear yours," she said.

"I'm not disappointed," I said. "Do you know why?"

"Why?" Margo asked obediently.

"Adam's always liked you. He's always noticed you. I don't think you'd have to work very hard to win him over, especially when he's in such a vulnerable state."

She came toward me sawing a finger in front of her lips. "April can hear everything we're saying!"

"She sleeps with a pillow over her head."

"You're assuming she's asleep. You're assuming I'd want to woo Adam and be inducted into his silly club!"

I've noticed that arguments can be won by substituting details where substance should be. "Not inducted. Welcomed. I'd do it, but April's told me he's freaked out by me."

"What about you?" Margo asked.

"My general demeanor, for some reason. Listen. Will you try?"

"If it'll make you happy . . . "

I thought about it. Not happy so much as satisfied, a less exalted feeling but infinitely more familiar.

The Re-enactors occupied a lovely brick building with white

columns and foul bathrooms in which eighteen-to-twenty-one-year-olds imbibed mixed drinks with a bravado that bordered on hysteria. I sipped beer out of a plastic cup, Margo by my side. Sometimes a fire burned in the fireplace and the little marble busts on the mantle were made to wear comedy and tragedy masks; on other occasions the hearth was cold and dead and the action of the party outside, above, on the roof and overloaded balconies. It was then I'd sit down, and listen to the distant raucous voices and try to discern which was April's, which Margo's (for she would have left me, been swept away by an admirer), and not be able to, and feel lonesomeness as a display of character, as if I were suffering onstage.

Club members had once performed events of decisive, even poetic, history: the first pebble cast by an Athenian in a democratic vote, Oppenheimer's disavowal of the nuclear bomb. But the charter had been amended, club dues reduced, the makeshift stage where reenactments had taken place fallen to a colony of termites. Now members were required only to reenact their own college years. Of course, they were still living out those years—but this was seen as a lucky coincidence, lending their performances authenticity and casting everything they said in a certain smart and dire light. They threw parties; they rehashed the particulars of the parties (carpets singed, a bathtub dropped off a third-floor balcony) in the lazy late hours of the next morning. Rumor had it that members of the Re-enactors recorded, in a black felt book with a quill pen, for future casting purposes, the approximate height and weight and outstanding physical characteristic of every single person who passed through the club's front doors. If that was true, I felt sure there was a question mark next to my notations. Why did I go to those parties, why pretend? I suppose it was for Margo (April drifted around in a cloud of members, supported and hemmed in). It was so she'd have somewhere to go. I didn't need it but she did. She was too kind to realize that, without me, she'd have had a much better time.

We had theories, certain suspicions. That a red hat worn on a member with brown hair meant something totally different than a blue hat worn on a member with blonde hair. That the haiku on the bathroom stalls contained directions to a cache of cocaine, and that the beautiful Scandinavian woman who circulated at every social event was actually a male philosophy professor. These were the things April had been poised to find out.

The last party we'd attended at the club was called Our Living Systems. It was an homage to biology class. The air smelled of formaldehyde, and on a low table in the middle of the main room was a set of ram's horns, some coral, and a wasp's nest like a massive, ruined wad of gum. A few mice had been released, the idea being that wherever there was biology class there were mice, little disease-bags. Margo and I were trying to capture them in order to take them outside and make them properly free. I didn't approve of this in-house wildness, not one bit.

Suddenly, Margo lurched toward a corner and held up a mouse by its tail. It seemed to swim in the air, and as its small paws paddled it gained a horizontal position. It sniffed ardently. I felt an explosion of sympathy.

"I'll take that." A boy called the Grouper for his recessed

chin and protuberant lower lip snatched the mouse away from her. He lowered it into a cup and turned the cup upside down on his head, and as the mouse scrabbled against his scalp a few drops of blood seeped out from under the rim and stood, lush as ink, on the ends of his hair. He smiled, beatific. Adam and April approached us.

"War paint!" Adam said.

The Grouper nodded soddenly.

April pinched my elbow. "You feel uncomfortable here, and so you take the rodents' side. Your heart just pours out to your fellow-oppressed."

She was exactly right. "Nonsense," I said.

"We were simply trying to release the mice into the wild," Margo said.

"I know *you* were," April answered.

The Grouper was the least attractive member of the Re-enactors and for that reason he was the physical jokester, the prank-player. Wiping blood from his brow, he took the cup off his head and pretended to swallow its contents. Adam frowned in disapproval, nodding toward me.

"I'm not the keeper of the animals," I said. "Do whatever you like."

"You're the keeper's conscience," Margo said.

"I'm nothing. I'm bored." I could feel my face turning red.

April began to laugh.

Next to a periodic table, a couple was dancing. They linked arms and dipped into and away from each other, smiling as if they meant it, which I suppose they did. Her velvet pants swirled about her legs, his jacket lapels flapped. Then he reached for her and lifted her above his head and began to twirl around and around and of course he dropped her, and that thud, the dead weight of it, its graceless determinacy, was an embarrassment to the evening. The girl made a sound like *ugh-hhna*. She was popular and bold, a photographer whose camera perched on the windowsill. Someone seized it and took her picture. Someone else took off her shoes—red Chinese slippers embroidered with mocking birds—and placed them on her head and took another picture. I left after that. The front porch was empty save for some sand-filled flowerpots in which cigarettes had been extinguished, and a ping-pong paddle mounded with shaving cream. I wondered what made the clacking sound in shaving cream cans, and if the sound grew louder as the can grew emptier. I wondered why Margo seemed to enjoy herself at these parties so much more than April did. When I'd announced that I was leaving, April had nodded in exhausted understanding, but Margo had given me an impertinent little wave. Her diffidence must mask a real yearning to be around people, while April was too practical to imagine a world in which she could be lonely. It just never occurred to her.

I walked home slowly. The university grounds were teeming with shadowy figures. Someone jumped up onto the railing of a pedestrian bridge and gesticulated wildly. Others were sunk together deep in laughter, like animals tearing at the same meat. During the day it would have been different, the grass would have cried out too brightly and the sunshine would have unmade our anonymity. But at night everyone was alone, whether they knew it or not.

When we told April what we were planning to do, she placed an olive in her mouth and worked the flesh away from the pit. "I can tell you right now what the ceremony's going to be like. A comic book." She spat into her hand. "You won't know where to look first."

I was sure this appealed to Margo. "What's important is that I inform you of the proceedings, that your feelings don't get hurt," I said.

"Why would my feelings be hurt by seeing my ex-boyfriend cavorting around with my roommate?"

"I don't know."

"Susan, have you ever been in love?" April asked.

We were in the kitchen. The olives glistened like the heads of seals.

"'Love comes from blindness, friendship from knowledge,'" I answered. "Someone said that. I forget who."

Margo opened the refrigerator and took a swig of ginger ale straight from the bottle. She burped resolvedly. "Where's Adam right now?"

April looked at her watch. "He's in class. He gets out at 11:50 and then he goes to the club to have lunch."

"Good. That's where I'll meet him." She pulled on a pair of black boots. They drooped around her ankles like a small child's stockings.

"Today's Wednesday," April called after her. "They'll be having watery minestrone!"

The front door slammed. Silence. A rearrangement of senses, the sort of pause that always accompanied such a thing.

I didn't know where to look. The day's instructions, the rules by which one lived, seemed suddenly inaccessible.

Then April said, "Adam enjoys portraying himself. His whole life's been spent in study. He used to freeze in front of the bathroom mirror, and make a face, and say, 'Therein lies bafflement.' Or, 'That dude right there is majorly hung over.'"

"Is he any good at it?"

"No. None of them are. They're mysteries inside, unapproachable. They know themselves only as replicas."

"Have you ever told him that?" I asked.

"Of course not."

"People can't always tell what you're thinking, you know."

"I depend on it," she said.

I met April and Margo in an archeology class. On a warm October morning we took a bus into the Virginia countryside, past horse farms and little churches and barns that looked like they'd been pried open with a crowbar. The fields were the yellow of sheets hung on a clothesline—a light-struck, light-stiffened color. Our bus passed a bicyclist in a slicker pedaling furiously down I-64. It wasn't raining. His slicker-wearing on a perfectly clear day struck me as foolish, and hopeful, in its preparedness. We stopped on the outskirts of Colonial Williamsburg and paced off the parameters of the dig, tying twine to wooden stakes and making a rectangle. "Go forth and find things," the professor said. A redheaded woman (April) was the first to step inside the twine lines. It was as if she were entering a real place, a country guided by some delicate anarchy, and had to act very quickly. She eschewed brushes and worked with her bare hands. The rest of us unearthed bullets but she discovered part of a pewter jug, and when she labeled and bagged it I saw her slip something else into her pocket. The leaves on the trees were high and bright and seeing that small theft gave me a feeling of freedom. On the way back to Charlottesville I sat next to her and asked her what she'd taken, but she wouldn't acknowledge my question until we were on campus walking away from the rest of the class. She looked over her shoulder to make sure we weren't being followed. Margo was right there. April beckoned her to fall in line with us and then drew out of her pocket a mesh ball on a chain. It looked like a tea strainer, but April said it was a pendant for filling with herbs and potions and casting spells.

"The colonists would grind anise and sage and burdock root, and place it in the pendant with gloved hands. They believed that if the potion came into contact with skin, the strength of the spell was sapped."

"They practiced witchcraft?" I asked.

"The women did," she said. "They saw it as their duty to keep the peace and allow the proper people to fall in love with each other."

"Historically, women were always doing things like that," Margo said.

"Like what?" I was annoyed by how close to me she was walking.

"Molding societies. Being deft shaping forces."

"She's right," April said.

We gossiped about our professor and the other students in the class as we walked the rest of the way to our dorms, which ended up being arranged just as we were on the sidewalk—April's on the end, mine in the middle, and Margo's on the other side—and at the end of that semester we left them and rented an apartment together.

Have I ever told you this? I imagined myself asking April. Once, I fell asleep to my radio and when I woke up Adam was dancing in my bedroom. His eyes were rolled back in his head and he was bouncing up and down on his toes. I pretended that I was still sleeping. He was wearing cut-off jeans and a T-shirt with a botanical rendering of poison ivy on it. His skin was as dense and pale as marble. It was the middle of the day. Have I ever told you this?

No, I imagined her answering. But when I say you weird Adam out I mean there is something obstreperous about you, something that refutes what it sees and argues incessantly with the world. You are the kind of person who has to be convinced of simple things, persuaded, dragged forth. You are an admonishment to ease.

Me: That doesn't explain what Adam was doing in my bedroom.

April: He was there to fluster you.

Me: He thought I was asleep!

April: No, he didn't.

But I never mentioned the incident to her, because I knew she'd have some way of making it a joke on me. Adam had a scar on his jaw from a skiing accident—April had struck him accidentally with one of her poles—and as he danced it gleamed, hook-shaped. His breathing was staccato and his chest was like a birdcage whose curved door shuddered outward, shuddered outward but never quite unlatched. As if it contained something it didn't want to let out. He bounced around for a few minutes and then darted from the room. I didn't know whether to laugh. Should I laugh? I asked his departing back. What were your intentions?

When Margo returned home after she'd gone to find Adam, I had to fight the urge to immediately ask her what happened. She needed some autonomy, to feel she was an equal partner in the operation. On the other hand, we only had a few days before the ceremony.

She brought a bag of baby carrots and a jar of peanut butter into the living room, where I was taking notes from a psychology textbook. Everyone else I knew toted along something to read while they ate, but not Margo. She dipped carrots in the peanut butter and took vigorous bites, staring into space.

"If people are waiting in two lines, one markedly longer than the other," I said, "did you know that a test subject will stand at the end of the longer line if the person in front of him does so too?"

"Confusion happens easily," she said.

I closed my book. "Oh?"

"Adam was very eager to talk about April. Their relationship was troubled, despite what we thought of it. That time April hit him in the face with her ski pole? He thinks it was deliberate."

I wasn't surprised. I could imagine doing all sorts of frustrated, covert things if I were in a relationship with someone like Adam. Someone whose privilege just begged to be undermined. "Where did you two talk?" I asked.

Margo began to unravel her braid. "In his room. He keeps things very neat. He's got a pencil holder shaped like Vincent van Gogh, and a jar of hard candies on his bookshelf."

"The authority you bring to this subject is quite remarkable, Margo," I said.

"Well, of course I'm going to remember the jar of candies," she said. "I was about to eat one when he kissed me." She withdrew from her pocket a half-wrapped butterscotch. The wrapper was sort of sheared away, as if it had come up against a great and roaring passion.

"This is ridiculous," I said, though I could not have explained why. I'd wanted the challenge, but maybe not the victory. Seeing my plan unfold was a way of glimpsing the future, and in doing so I realized how unnatural that was. There are certain barriers, shields smooth as silk, that aren't meant to be perforated. Time was one of those.

"You're the matchmaker," Margo reminded me.

"I know," I said. "I'm in it now."

As I rode my bicycle downtown, its chain rattling, I wondered where the man in the rain slicker had been going that day I saw him from the bus window, the day of the archeology class outing. I hadn't thought about him in over a year, but I could still see his bent billowing figure, his spinning legs. Despite all his effort, the bus had overtaken him easily. Its speed seemed monstrous in retrospect, and the man's endeavoring pure and doomed. Once our bus had passed him he'd been surrounded by a new fleet of vehicles, and I'd lost sight of him before I wanted to.

I locked my bike to a parking meter and went into a clothing store full of circulating undergraduates. Margo already had lots of dresses, mostly vintage, frowsy things, but I figured she could use something new for the Re-enactors' ceremony. The dresses I examined were brilliant, bound for spacious closets and dabbings of lemon and fizzy water should they become stained. "Does this frock convey a spunky moneyed imperturbability?" I imagined someone asking a saleslady. Margo and I were approximately the same height, though she was thinner. I chose a pale green dress with a plunging neckline, tried it on, and paid for it with a check.

April was sitting on the curb in front of the store. She must have followed me there. She took off her headphones, letting them encircle her neck, and stood to extend her hand. "Here." She pried open my palm. "You deserve this. It didn't work for me."

The pendant was stuffed with something odorous. "What do you mean?"

"I tried to set Adam and Justine up. But nothing happened." Justine did maintenance for our apartment building, tending to running toilets and sniffing out gas leaks on stoves.

"Justine is a married Southeast Asian woman of indeterminate age," I said.

"All the same," replied April, "the power of the pendant is dwindling." She sighed deeply. "When I used to imagine my college years, they were certainly not tinged by such inconsequentiality."

"You're important to your friends."

"Friends? You mean conspirators? You and Margo have a

terrible kind of curiosity." April shook her head. "Yet without it, where would you be?"

The sidewalk sparkled with whatever made cement sparkle.

"Nowhere?" I asked.

"Farther away than that," she said.

The night of the ceremony, Margo put on the green dress and waited for Adam in her bedroom. I was downstairs with April. It was raining, and I walked over to the window. The streetlights seemed to concentrate and isolate the downpour, as if their cylindrical heads were rain clouds. When Adam pulled up in an old gray Mercedes, an aristocratic cast-off of his father's, I was sure he would honk. Instead, he came inside.

"Neanderthal!" April said. We were playing Scrabble. She laid down the L.

Adam was wearing a tuxedo shirt and a pair of pinstriped pants. "Good word," he said.

"Apt, don't you think?"

"Don't be mad, April."

"I'm not mad. My brain is revving."

"Don't rev it at me."

April dug in the bag for more tiles. The sound was a small consolation.

Margo came downstairs and got into her raincoat. She wasn't wearing her glasses. Her face was painted and arranged for being on display. Her feet in their black ballet flats were going to get soaked. They were going to leave sopping prints on the club floor. "Okay," she said, when she'd zipped herself up. April would've left the coat undone, the better to frame her beauty.

Once, when I was a child, I saw my mother approach the bathroom where my father was taking a bath with a carton of orange juice in her hand. Although she shut the door behind her, I heard him exclaim as she poured the cold juice in. I was reminded now of the way antipathy between two people created a kind of alternate room in which the others, if there were others, found themselves stranded. But of course, in the case of April and Margo, I'd built that room myself.

Adam shook loose the folds of his umbrella and gently prodded Margo forward with its tip.

When I woke the next morning I knew right away that Margo hadn't returned from the ceremony and that I'd have to go get her. The apartment was very still and shadowed and expectant. April was asleep on the couch, snoring softly. Outside, the pavement was damp from last night's rain.

What can I do? I thought the whole way to the club. I'd never been there alone before. I came with nothing and was looking for something. I came with nothing.

The bushes in front of the large brick building were decorated with paper flowers. Inside, I found the members drinking mimosas. They greeted me with elaborate courtesy. "Good morning, Susan," they said. "Have a croissant, have something to drink." They surrounded me, forcing me backwards, deeper and deeper into the chambers, as if I were being carried along by a wave whose strength I had underestimated. They possessed a tangled innocence, a gravelly purity. A little stubble sat softly on their faces. The Grouper approached me.

"Delighted to see you," he said.

"Tell me where Adam and Margo are."

"They're rejoicing."

"In what?"

"In the rejoicing room."

I realized he was drunk. "You're no help at all."

"Listen, we're all here to have a good time. Why aren't you, Sue? Why aren't you ever here to have a good time?"

"I don't know."

"Clearly not." The Grouper sniffed. "You obviously don't know how. It's not a skill. It's not even a decision."

"I think I might scream," I said.

"Go ahead. She won't hear you."

I howled her name and a directive to come get me, and then something much less reasoned. The Grouper grasped my shoulders and forced me to sit on a couch dusty with pool chalk. Across the room, someone had written *duct tape* on the wall with duct tape. A chandelier hung like a dismantled star from a wire in the ceiling.

Adam crossed the room to me surprisingly quickly, though it seemed he was hardly moving at all. His tuxedo shirt was half unbuttoned, the frills flattened and sides spread, making a deep V of his skin. He took my hand. "There's no reason for this," he said. "Calm down."

"Tell me what happened at the ceremony last night," I said.

"We quoted each other and drank cocktails. That's all we do."

I'd expected more than a group of winsome-looking people standing around and pretending to be refined, then devolving gratifyingly, inexorably, into their usual strewn selves. I'd thought members might have re-created for the girlfriends in question moments of love's recognition, capture, containment. "No performances? No special rituals?"

"No, just special punch with special vodka." He began to laugh, and his scar shone again. I waited for him to say something else. I wanted him to keep holding my hand in his articulate, grasping way. Instead, he tugged at it.

I followed.

Margo wasn't anywhere I could see. But the pencil-holder, the jar of candies, a bunk bed whose lower mattress had been turned on end and propped against the top bunk, creating a slide like a person would use to escape from an airplane—all of this was very clear to me. I could see myself lying on Adam's bed with him so close to the ceiling, kissing, engaging in that grievous kind of wrestling that occurs between two people, and Adam drawing away . . .

"Margo wants you to have this," he said, putting a garbage bag in my hand. Inside was the dress I'd bought, lithesome and irrelevant in black plastic.

He was a mouth-breather. He sucked in slushy air.

Downstairs. Members were still drinking in the anteroom, their tousled heads bent over their cups. They were like a field of sheep glimpsed from a touring car's window—matching, remote creatures who simply did what they were meant to do. Outside, the paper flowers were bleeding onto the bushes. For a moment I thought I couldn't go home. It was the bigness of the bag and the little collapse of fabric. It was something soft and hopeful in the dark enclosure of the world. Then I remembered the dumpster around back, and I went to it and tossed the bag in. It landed noiselessly on the noisy junk.

April was still on the couch in her pajamas, her hair pulled back with the kind of low-grade rubber band that comes wrapped around free newspapers.

"I'm starving," I announced. "How about you?"

"I could be convinced."

We got in the car and I drove us to the part of town with the chain restaurants where we could have any old greasy thing. April stared away from me, out her window. We came to a car dealership whose vehicles filled a parking lot, humped roofs stretching in replicated rows up and down, right and left. The cars were blinking. Their hazard lights were on, blinking all at once, and the longer they did so the more in accordance they grew until it appeared that they were perfectly synchronized. The lights were crisp and red and seemed to possess multiply a single vibrant intent. Traffic slowed and then stopped. "It's like they're timed," April said.

"Like they've got life," I said.

"Got life? You mean *alive?*"

"No, like they've *got life,*" I insisted. "It's temporary." An artificial state, an uncanny endowment. Beautiful cars.

The years would make us strange to each other. The pattern would shift, become variegated, soft. Like Morse code for the deaf, little messages sewn with electric thread. Traffic started moving again. We left the flickering behind.

The Help

My nurse fell asleep taking a few deep breaths, like the steps that lead from the deck of a swimming pool into the water. I stayed awake what felt like most of the night, but was probably twenty- or thirty-minute patches here and there. Each time I opened my eyes I felt a weird alertness, as if I were taking a test. The sky was the color of milk in a blue plastic glass. In the morning, my nurse—whose uniform was stitched above the right-hand breast pocket with *Bobbie Blunt*—rose from the recliner and smoothed out her skirt. Her hair, pressed to the side of her head with frazzled wisps escaping, resembled the casually baroque style of many of the current movie stars. She told me I passed a restful night, that the expression on my face was first puzzled and then knowing, then placid, then beautiful. She was lying, of course, but I didn't mind.

She brought breakfast, lunch, and dinner to me, positioning the trays in order of consumption. "What are you going to do today?" she asked as she packed the blood pressure cuff and digital thermometer into her black bag.

"Oh, I don't know. Gather myself. Prepare."

She glanced around the barren room. "Really?" she said.

"Looks like you're ready."

She'd never seen the basement, where I stowed most of my belongings when I came so close to dying. A waffle iron, dots of batter still stuck to its surface. A picnic hamper packed with rolled change and shearing scissors, a spiky clutch of ear-rings and a French press, all the breakable, inessential things I tended to first, in the confusion.

Bobbie laced her spongy-soled shoes. When she left, I waved at the last minute too vigorously. She didn't see me and I was chagrined at my own enthusiasm.

"Nurse!" I called.

The door shut but the screen stayed open—she'd paused, probably rummaging in her purse for the keys to her minivan, an unsteady looking vehicle with the wobbly tires of a ten-speed—making the half-exhalation it did when the delivery man propped a package there. I ordered almost everything: medical encyclopedias, sheets and pillowcases patterned with peonies (my favorite flower—they look exploded). The objects on my bedside table, those closest to me—water glass and jug, crossword puzzle, whatever book I was reading (usually a tale of family outrages written by the daughter of someone famous)—had acquired the bearing of items at a shrine, like the notes, class rings, and pictures of dead schoolchildren that mourners left behind, to have something to return to, presumably. Why did they all look alike, those capsized kids with their quick dark hair? Bravery and foolishness and some bony, remote quality linked them to each other, to their foreshortened fates.

The screen door closed. I wondered what she would do if her van didn't start, who she'd call. Oh nurse, I thought—for

I couldn't bring myself to call her Bobbie, a stiff and sugary name—to what steady liberty is your life dedicated? Do ideas pulse inside you like toothaches?

But the van started. She drove away.

When I finished breakfast I decided to sit in the sun for a little while. I carried a plastic container of water outside, filled the birdbath, and lowered myself into a lawn chair. In the next yard, my neighbor was talking on the telephone. "My mom always told me, 'Cut your gelatin into cubes. Never give away something that you've gotten as a gift. A prayer lasts at least three full minutes.' She was full of cute ideas." She raised her arm over her head and waved at me. "Nice to see you out!" she called.

I waved back, just a little motion, like I was trying to cool off a forkful of food. The water in the birdbath shone dully. I remembered reading somewhere that the female mosquito needed a blood meal before she could lay her eggs, that it prepared the eggs for the challenge of being deposited in a thin film of dirty water, emboldened them, gave them strength. The phrase *blood meal* made me suspicious of the writer's authority, for he seemed to revel in it, as if to make his subject more exciting. If I closed my eyes I could still see how it dotted the pages of the text, following rapidly upon illustrations of the glowing mosquito and tubular, stalwart eggs.

Five months ago, the blood in my leg stopped moving. It formed a clot and traveled to my lungs. I was taking a shower when I stopped being able to breathe; I batted the curtain aside and staggered out of the water, my hair coated with papaya shampoo. It seemed as if my supply of air, formerly bountiful, lay now in one or two shimmering drops deep in the cavity of my chest. I thought I might faint before I put my clothes back on, so I wrapped myself in a towel. I dialed 911 and the air came in a hazy contrail.

The emergency room nurse gave me an IV of Heparin, an anticoagulant. Then she ran a dye through my arms and torso and took a CT scan to locate the clot. The pictures that came back showed a ribcage with a rosebud crushed against it.

I had to return to the hospital every two weeks to check the clotting factor in my blood. I couldn't eat anything with vitamin K in it. My chest sang with remembered pain. That's when I hired a nurse.

Tonight, Bobbie arrived at 9:13. She sighed as she sat down beside the bed. Then there was silence, not the ordinary kind but something as tactile as an iced-over phone line. She took out some knitting, a lumpy scarf of furious purples and pinks with an uneven, Charlie Brown zig-zag down the middle.

"How do you feel?" she asked finally. "Circulation any better?"

"Not really. The clot isn't risky anymore, but it stays where it is."

"That's terrible. You have to walk around with it?" She paused and seemed to consider something. "Come with me."

She strapped me into the backseat of the minivan, made a series of turns (I closed my eyes to avert car sickness) and then began driving in one direction. I opened my eyes again. We were on the highway, traveling side-by-side with other vehicles at the same rough speed; I could see, for a few hyper-illuminated seconds, the occupants of the cars that surrounded us. They looked beatific and a little drugged, staring out from under their bangs at the swift black road. Exits appeared and then disappeared, as if the destination itself were gone. Bobbie maneuvered the minivan determinedly, with both hands at the top of the steering wheel. She left the highway and a few minutes later pulled into the parking lot of a doughnut shop, a low brick building the size of which seemed to be doubled by its outpouring of light. Stepping from the van, I could smell the sugar coming from the ventilation system, as if a cake were being mixed by the fan's huge blades.

The people streaming into the shop wore baggy pants and had rounded white faces like the helms of boats. There was a feeling in the air of repressed memories resurfacing; of a hunger, just a tiny bit melancholy, breaking free. Those emerging carried polka-dotted boxes that they propped on the hoods of their cars, opened the lids, and began to eat rapidly from.

"You can watch the doughnuts come down the line here, all fresh and hot," Bobbie said. "This is a popular sight. I wanted you to see it."

We joined the crowd in the shop. Glazed doughnuts traveled three abreast along a black conveyor belt. At the end of the belt, workers boxed the doughnuts with hands encased in clear plastic.

A girl in front of us plucked a doughnut off the belt. She bit into it, making whimpering sounds and flapping her hand in front of her mouth.

"She's eating a hotter doughnut than anyone has a right

to," Bobbie said. "It's like looking into something before it's even got an inside."

The girl's mother paid for her daughter's doughnut, unapologetic, and then we paid for ours and went back to the van. Bobbie leaned against the door and ate one doughnut and I lay across the backseat and ate four. Flakes of glaze fell onto my face like sticky, resolute snow. Bobbie looked into the car and smiled absently. I could hear the strange music of the cash register every time the shop door opened to admit another customer. And snatches of conversation, a man saying *I'm going to need three Boston Cremes,* as if he was preparing to operate under a punishing imperative.

"Do you have to go?" I asked Bobbie in the morning.

"I've got other patients to see," she said. "Clients, I mean. I'm supposed to refer to you as my client."

"Aren't I your friend?" How squinty, how desperate a question.

"Well, that's another procedural change." Bobbie jabbed her thumb in the direction of the ceiling. "The powers that be tell us not to get too friendly with our clients. Excursions should be educational, they say. Taking you to the doughnut shop was a bit of a stretch. We're supposed to go places like museums and libraries, or tour factories that, and I quote from the handbook, "*manufacture harmless substances and provide innocuous, distracting souvenirs.*"

"I suppose it's so you don't get too close to someone who might die," I said.

Bobbie shook her head. "Nurses are used to that sort of

thing. Death. It's almost trivial. It's so the patients—rather, clients—don't get too attached to us."

"Has that ever happened to you? Has one of your patients gotten too clingy?"

"A man left me an envelope with forty single dollar bills in it, one for each year of his life."

I imagined Bobbie picking up the envelope and gazing into it eagerly as if it might contain a bit of white powder. Just a snort, some dying man's last generosity.

"That was nice of him," I said.

"His records stated that he was forty-five." She turned to go. "He owes me, but who would I complain to?"

Once every few months, I was supposed to meet with the chief of nurses—Bobbie's boss—to talk about my treatment plan, but lately I'd been putting it off. I was expected to have concerns about her, to raise objections. If not, I wasn't taken seriously as a patient. Under the lopsided gaze of the chief of nurses I found myself fabricating small incidents designed to show just enough displeasure with the care I was getting to be plausible, but not enough to cause him to assign a different nurse to me. It was a trying situation. In order to lie effectively, some part of me had to believe what I was saying.

The day arrived, after repeated phone calls from his office, when I couldn't delay going in any longer. I arrived in a wheelchair (a prop I used only occasionally). The furniture in the waiting room was pushed too close together to easily accommodate it, forcing me to weave awkwardly in and out of the magazine rack and coffee table and couch. I began to pant. The chief of nurses called my name just as I was slipping some glossy magazines into the wheelchair's back pocket (a little bonus I believed I was entitled to, for all my work). I ran the obstacle course again, only backwards, and wheeled myself into his office.

He sat waiting. On the wall behind his desk was a child's drawing of a man sitting at a desk. Written at the bottom was DAD UR SO ONBARSEG.

"Deep vein thrombosis," I began. "A traffic jam of the blood. Some days, I can't feel myself at all. My body's more like a space than an entity."

"Not to be rude, but"—he made a series of small scoops with his hand—"etc., etc., etc. What I really want to talk to you about is Bobbie."

"What about her?"

He shrugged. "Just go ahead and dish."

I opened my hands in a but-I-have-nothing gesture.

"Haven't you two moved beyond the purely professional? Don't you gossip at all?"

"She said that was against the rules."

"Totally ignorable," the chief of nurses said. "Just policy. Bobbie should know that. She should get the drift."

"Maybe she sees things she doesn't want to talk about," I said.

"Like what? A baby picking scabs out of its own hair? An elderly person saying her bladder's a casket of refined wine? You see stuff in this profession. You laugh at it."

"She doesn't."

"She's so infuriatingly respectful," the chief of nurses said.

"I want to be respected by her, but she's too busy respecting other things."

On his desk, an apple-shaped kitchen timer went off with a long buzz.

As I wheeled myself home, the drivers of cars idling at red lights looked curiously in my direction. I thought I must be using the wheelchair wrong. I let my head drop to my chest, and when I looked back up, a man in a black truck continued to scrutinize me. His tongue protruded from the little hole of his mouth like a fingertip from a pair of ripped gloves. When the light changed he popped his tongue back in and drove off with a series of anarchic honks. I abandoned the chair in the parking lot of a liquor store—tipped over, plastic padded blue seat with hospital serial number stamped on back, wheels still spinning—and walked the rest of the way.

There was a knock at the door. My mother let herself in, and told me to lie back down. She brought me a glass of orange juice with ice.

"It practically tastes like another drink this way," she said.

I propped a pillow under my head and took a sip. The ice bobbed rudely against my top lip.

"Tell me something about my childhood," I said.

She patted her pockets. "But I don't have my little cream-colored book."

"Can't you remember anything?"

"Oh, let's see. Once, you rescued a turtle from under the wheels of an ice cream truck. All the other children were at the window ordering their treats. I looked at what you were doing, standing back, evaluating you as a small human being and not my daughter at all, and I realized that your concern was only for yourself. You did not want to have to witness the turtle's suffering. But the turtle was already dead."

She was smiling as if she didn't realize what she was saying. I fought off a swell of nausea by imagining a bucket bringing cold, cold water up from a well. "How's Gram?"

Mother dug in her bag. "She wanted me to give you this card."

I turned past the lacy cover to my grandmother's handwriting, well-cut but seemingly temporary, like the lines skates make on fresh ice. *I'll see myself to the door, thanks. Which one of us is going?*

"What does she mean by that?" I asked.

"What does she mean by what?" Mother said, giggling.

"Has Gram forgotten who I am?"

She shook her head. "She's selected to let certain memories expire. She's an old woman. She has room for just so much."

I sat up abruptly and spilled my drink. The carpet caught the ice cubes and held them on its fiber-ends.

"She doesn't actually like me, does she? She never has!"

"That's not true. Gram used to love to shampoo you, and give you a good cream rinse. She'd put on a plastic apron and shampoo you for hours. She'd just shampoo and shampoo. You'd sit there with foam lumped on your head and in your ears, looking at me like there was something wrong with having your own Gram shampoo you. I think you became sickly then, and never got over it."

The house we lived in was always chilly, even in the summertime. It seemed a steam rose from the carpet, like a bog, and the wallpaper glittered with condensation. Gram kept the drapes drawn, and then hung quilts over them because she didn't think they were heavy enough.

"Don't you have any help around here?" Mother asked, looking up and down the room. "Haven't you hired a lady for that?"

"No," I said. "It's just me."

Bobbie's van turned into the driveway with a sound like the cement being whipped. Nurse, who are you? I thought. Our outing to the doughnut shop brought us closer, I could tell, but it also solidified her doubts about me. Doubts that she probably felt bad about having and were all the stronger that way.

When she came into my bedroom, she was sweating.

"What's wrong?" I asked.

"It's nothing. Try to get to sleep."

"I want to talk. Will you talk to me?"

In the shadows her face looked vague, as if she were a statue that had been mostly demolished.

"What do you want to talk about?" she asked.

"I don't know. My funeral arrangements. I have very particular ideas about what I want to happen on that day."

She reached for a pad of paper and a pen. "Let it rip."

"Mauve and silver bunting. A roomful of teary, overdressed people. Platters of smoked cheeses. The coffin should be closed and at least one person should try to pry it open. Coming through the windows, the sounds of traffic and children playing street hockey."

Bobbie was smiling. "You really know what you want, don't you?"

"About this, I do."

"Better that than nothing."

"It's sort of morbid."

"Every obsession is," she said.

"Do you think I'm obsessed with dying?" I asked.

"I think you're obsessed with being sick. Dying would put an end to it, wouldn't it? But being sick can last you a long, long time."

I closed my eyes. I could hear Bobbie shifting around in her chair a little more than usual, as if debating the merits of what she'd said.

A couple of hours went by.

"You're right," I said to the body sleeping next to me.

Mother announced that she and Gram were moving to a retirement community in Arizona called Heron's Landing. She came over to say goodbye.

"I reminded her of who you are," she said, handing me another card.

I opened it slowly. Pasted to the top of the card, in letters cut from the newspaper, was the heading *A NeW StArt*. Beneath that, Gram had written *My dear, I did not mean confuse you. I am going to live in a very small room, in a very small to room with your mother.*

I remembered, at a holiday dinner, Gram lifting a handkerchief to her mouth, dabbing at the corners and then placing the handkerchief inside and beginning to chew. A stubborn, displeased look came over her face when she realized what she'd done, but she kept chewing and chewing, her jaw working hard, until she turned her head and, like a magician, drew the handkerchief out.

I lobbed the card onto my bedside table. "Well, Gram seems resigned to a somewhat limited new life," I said. "I'll probably never see her again, so tell her . . ."

"No, not small at all," Mother interrupted. She crossed her legs and wagged her foot, her plastic sandal dangling from her toes, which resembled a descending line of big-headed, armless clay people. "Dunes of people where the desert used to be. Cheap pink Mexican pastries."

"I'm glad you two are finally doing what you want."

"Gram doesn't want. Gram is an empty vehicle which I shall gas up and ride, ride across the country."

"That's a nice way to put it."

Mother got up and paced around the room. "Saguaro salt-and-pepper shakers, sunsets that linger so long you just want to turn the sky off." She snapped her head around. "Question."

"Go ahead."

"I've been wanting to ask you, since you're closer to the . . . edge than anyone I know, closer than Gram, maybe . . ."

"It's okay, Mother. What is it?"

She lowered her voice. "When you're just a soul, will you come to me and tell me things I couldn't otherwise know?"

I thought of all that was hidden becoming revealed. Revealed, it would just sit there, inappropriately sending out signals.

"Please?"

"I'll never be a soul. I'm too heavy," I said.

The chief of nurses was stretched across one of the couches in his waiting room, his arm flung across his eyes. I sat down across from him, carrying peanut butter-and-honey sandwiches that Bobbie had made. The rustling of the bag made him sit up, yawn, shake his disheveled head.

"No wheelchair?" he asked, as he accepted a sandwich.

"No. I crawled here. It took a while."

He smiled and bit into the bread with a sudden avian motion, and when he pulled away there was a piece of crust hanging from his mouth. He let the crust drop into his lap and then flicked it over his shoulder, where I knew there was no garbage can.

"I came here to tell you about my dream," I said. "I was being examined by specialists, poked and prodded and all my symptoms penciled into charts. Then we decided to walk downtown, me trailed by the specialists, and we stopped in a bookstore with a Saint Bernard lying across the floor. And it seemed that the great dog was lying on all the books I wanted to read. I just couldn't find anything on the shelves. But the specialists could, they found armfuls of books. That's when I knew they would succeed and I wouldn't. They were interested in the world."

"Trippy," he said.

"Yeah."

We chewed our sandwiches. The stippled fabric of the waiting room chair scratched pleasantly against the backs of my legs.

"You have to let go," he said finally. "Give your body up to someone else. The safeguarding of it, the maintenance, everything. Just forget about it."

"Impossible," I said.

"Do you think I worry about"—he looked down at himself—"this? Do you actually think I spend one second of the day contemplating the state of myself?"

"But that's the duty of your profession."

"To care for others, yes. But for me?" He laughed. "Not a chance. It's a kind of forgetfulness, nursing is. You forget yourself when you're doing it. At the end of your shift, after all the coughs and shunts and clammy skin, when you go back to your apartment, oh how precious it is. Everything just as you left it. No syringes, no blood sugar tests."

I nodded. I could imagine the relief of that.

Bobbie was rustling through my medicine cabinet, popping pills. I didn't have anything very strong—Tylenol P.M., Extra Strength something else—but she was looking for more, I could tell she thought there may be more. I imagined the chalky pills, three or four of them, cupped in the bowl of her hand. I glanced at the bedside clock. It was the middle of the night.

"Nurse," I said softly. "Do you want to rest?"

She appeared in the doorway. I got out of bed and she lay down.

In the kitchen, I opened the refrigerator and stared at its contents. There was a small spill of maple syrup. My mouth was dry. I thought about flushing the pills down the toilet, but instead I went into the bathroom and swept the containers off the shelves of the medicine cabinet into the sink. Then I carried them, a little damp, into the dining room and arranged them on the table and sealed their lids with tape. I wondered if the gesture's half-finality made it hopeful or hopeless.

User! I thought now when I served Bobbie a meal. Artificially desirous! But Bobbie had no appetite. She didn't like the loft of my pillows or that you could see fingerprints on my ceiling, something I'd always thought rather lovely and strange. She answered the phone when my mother called, and hung up as Mother said (I knew, because I was on the other extension), "Hold everything. What's wrong with your voice?" On the fifth day, I returned from the grocery and found Bobbie stripping the bed. She looked up a little wild-eyed at my approach.

"I guess I got home earlier than you expected?" I said.

She nodded glumly. "I thought I'd have time. I thought it would be easier this way."

I remembered her ironing out the skirt of her uniform with the palms of her hands. It was wrinkled now, an affront to itself. "How do you feel?" I asked.

"Fine. And you?"

"Well," I said, meaning *well, there are conditions to what I'm about to say,* but she didn't allow me to go on. She gave a little twirl as she dropped the dirty sheets on the floor.

"I cured you!" she said.

"No."

"I did, I did." She laughed. "You just can't feel it yet."

One of the last times I went to the hospital for tests, I heard two women gossiping about another woman they knew. They were standing in a bathroom in the hospital's hematology/oncology wing; I was in a stall. Their friend had cut herself while slicing a cantaloupe, one of them said, and then, inexplicably, she wouldn't stop bleeding.

"The royal disease," the other said.

The first woman snorted. "Remember who we're talking about."

The crook of my arm felt tender and itchy from having blood drawn. I unwrapped my bandage because it had been put on too tightly. A single spot of red showed through the gauze pad. A gift to have so much of it—moving, flowing, pushing the body's codes forward, upward. Bringing messages into various chambers, pure demands.

There was the whirr of paper towels being dispensed. "Imagine watching it happen," the first women said. "Wondering when it was going to stop."

"I bet she wasn't thinking of anything of end-importance."

"She couldn't have been. They got to her in the nick of time. But the thing is"—here the voice lowered, and I had to strain to hear what was being said—"she's not grateful for it. She's almost the opposite. Always like, why me? She's like someone who maybe shouldn't have—I don't want to say *survived,* but there you have it—because she just doesn't appreciate how lucky she is."

I began wrapping the bandage around my arm again.

"You can say it," her friend assured her. "You can say survived."

Privations

Los Angeles

The lily pads are gone, gone, and this is less a worry than a verdict: sad. They've all died on the lake in Echo Park. Or is it lotus leaves? I can't remember. I read about it in the newspaper, a neighborhood's minor tragedy, but it feels larger to me. Pollution to blame, probably. I don't remember that part either, just the fact of flora, which I suppose I read as possibility, being replaced by the absence of flora. The blossoms, in pictures, like silken briefly crumpled handkerchiefs. They used to be the pride of Echo Park. Soon our planet will be full of the dead habits of people.

Places of Origin

"I'm nearly hysterical with tiredness," I say to Alexis, and by her silence on the other end of the line I know this was a mistake. She does not want to hear it. Her father sits in front of his computer all day, composing his op-eds ("The Olympics Must Return To Their Hellenic Birthplace," "The Disappearance of African Grains and Pulses"), but still she does not want to hear about how I have to do every little thing. She lives in Portland and thinks her life began last year, the correct manifestation of her life. A dark woman with inflexible eyes, a body winnowed to long and balanced bones by mountain bike rides. I start to tell her a story about something Leo did, just a little anecdote, but she interrupts me. "Divorce him," she says. Her brusqueness a gate barring people like me from more varied parts of her personality. I can't divorce Leo. He'd drown without me, in American exigencies, in automated telephone systems and police charity fundraisers and the other kinds of transactions that require a diplomacy and patience the boy from the Greek village came unequipped with. I am the girl from the Ohioan village. I am, like I said, nearly hysterical.

Gridlock

Considering the automobile: gleaming steel, tires from which air may be constantly leaching . . . How will our roads accommodate us? I listen to the traffic report on the radio and the woman's voice says, "SIG alert on the 405," and I do not need to know what "SIG" stands for to know it's bad. Sudden Illogical Gap? Shit In Groves? My car tries to tell me what it needs. Lights and signs flash to life on the dashboard. Fluid low. Door ajar. Airbags off again (a suicidal impulse). Stop and go. Slow and go. There's a coziness to its interior, the kind of coziness one might attribute to a dog house. Pal loves it in his little plastic igloo! Pal would feel *lost* without his wet-cardboard-sweaty-baby-shoe-super-glue-smelling igloo. (Hoping it's not cruel, hoping he's not lonely.) The faces of my fellow commuters as expressionless as cheese, for who can admit to being themselves caught in such ridiculous traffic? I try making eye contact with the fellow next to me: middle-aged, hand on steering wheel hairy and heavily ringed, the hair sprouting from between and beneath the rings like a paw or a claw or a talon banded to be counted by wildlife officials. His coincidental proximity, the miniature hula dancer vibrating on his dashboard . . . I am suddenly irrevocably attracted to him. He thinks I want to merge, and waves me in.

Barricade

My brother won't let me inside his house. He's always been private, but I suspect something worse. An adolescent boy wearing a loincloth tied up in a bamboo pen. Piles of pornography and ancient drugs. I don't know. Teddy's smart—he taught himself Old English, the sitar, hydroponics. Took the interesting things from the world for himself. Then came a subtle change. Cartons of heavy cream in his recycling container. He started to smoke again, and his little dog lost her fur and had to go on a diet of kangaroo meat. Kangaroo meat was the only thing she could eat. Anyway, when I used to be allowed inside, I'd rest uneasily on the edge of some soiled chair and wonder how one person could be so messy. It was like an orphanage of reprobates in there. Yet an element of jealousy clung to my condemnation, because Teddy lived wholly for himself and maybe for the idea of himself that fluttered about him like a wide-girthed angel. Or, even more possibly, for the idea of extricating himself from everything. Rolling in the red carpet, locking the door. We are siblings, strangers. This is okay by him.

Appetite

Bill Clinton is standing outside Curves. I've just finished my circuit, but luckily I'm not sweating. "Come on over," he says, extending his hand. He looks less jovial than he used to, more desperate. I extend my hand, pull it back. "Don't be nervous," he says. I reach out my hand again and he takes it. Marsupial warmth. His thumb licks my palm. Bulbous nose, mop of white hair, a voice like scummy honey—he's a puppet on Sesame Street, the adult version. We have all fallen the way he has fallen. Less publicly, perhaps, un-televised, un-transcribed, but great shame has come upon all of us in the viewing audience. Bill and I go out for milkshakes. Strawberry and chocolate malt, so thick we can hardly coax the stuff up a straw. His flirtation dissipates in the presence of the big silver cups. He wants to try mine, but doesn't let me try his, and this inequality feels very familiar. The old rage begins. I want to offer to his sucking face profound sociological observations. The slackness of men inures them against the details! Women make lists in their heads, and then their heads become the lists they make, a chicken scratch catalogue of need. The fair sex's oeuvre. Instead, I get one of those cold beverage headaches.

A Pirate's Life

My husband's chest hair is like primal graffiti: nature was here. Shirtless, often, even at fifty. He called Clarence Thomas a nigger. He must be given prompt refills of coffee. Will he remember to take the dog out? Close the windows? Can he be trusted to be the one at home when a repair guy comes over? My body thrums with frustration (a helpless motor) when he interrupts me, yell-yawns as I'm trying to get to sleep. Once, on a "pirate" boat ride we were taking with the kids, he leapt across my lap to wrench an aerosol can of sunscreen from a stranger's hand.

I didn't know if it was the ozone-depleting aerosol he objected to, or its proximity to us, or the fat and busy way the woman was whizzing the can back and forth over her son. All of the above, most likely, a final abomination in a tally he was keeping. I tried my best to shield Jason and Alexis from the spectacle, but I'm sure they saw everything: the woman calling for the captain, Leo's scolding, the other passengers' faces like the faces of blank nobility.

Foreign Languages

Body surfing on vacation in Greece—the wave approaching, tucking perfectly into itself, and I was flying, tumbling, scraping, the bottom of the ocean gritty with stuff you'd think would be soggy, but wasn't. As if wetness doesn't exist underwater. A sharp pain in my neck. I crawled to shore, where the children were building a sandcastle and Leo was sitting with his sister, smoking a cigarette. "I hurt my neck," I said. His sister smiled. "Nice, eh?" "No, I"—pointing to my neck—"crack." She shrugged her shoulders. Leo said something to her. "Ah!"—and as she began to jabber excitedly in Greek it was as if I could understand everything. *Listen, bedraggled wife of my brother, should we go get your hair done? Some new clothing? Golden rings? Why be alive if you can't be a woman? Leave the sea alone.* And I wondered if she, in turn, could comprehend me. *I stuff all that gaudy shit you give me in the back of the closet when I get home.* She laughed and clapped her hands, a queen on an island of rocks. *You are preposterous!* I couldn't look to the right or to the left. I could only look straight ahead.

Sleight of Hand

I sense that I'm learning less and less about my son. It's like the game with the three overturned cups, one of which has a ball beneath. I always guess the wrong one. He is a writer for a technology website. What does that even mean? I don't want to be maudlin. Yes, I do—Jason was such an easy, happy baby. Each young year broke upon him with its treats: fire engines, superheroes and their capes and shields. Alexis came along later, but for a little while it was just us. I'd pick him up and he'd fit himself into my side. I'd kiss his soft face. He snored like a drunken bee. Then the inevitable shifting of allegiances—a roughening, a secret drumming inside of him. I couldn't any longer predict what he needed. The sidelong smiles of girls, probably, their hair like the pennants of winning teams. I feared he was lonely, and that his desires would not move beyond what he himself could provide. Crackly T-shirts stuffed deep in his dirty laundry attested to that. You have to strive for happiness, I thought, seeing him not strive. Now I know technology can mean anything from microchips to wheelchair lifts to missile defense systems. Website is the thing you bring up on your computer screen. My son is the words there.

What's in a Name

Leo = lion. Equals 13 popes, 6 Byzantine emperors, 5 Armenian kings. Famous Russian novelist. Constellation (most triumphant of connect-the-dots). Leo in the world vs. Leo at home. He can be charming with other people. Kisses women on both cheeks, claps their husbands on their backs, speaks knowledgeably about the internment of Japanese during World

War II, the plight of black farmers, the death of polytheism to the demands of Christianity. But if I try to interject, he commands, "Wait your turn!" Or makes a skeptical "Aaaaghh" sound and tells me to be quiet. Still, I don't want our dinner companions' sympathy. I avoid their eyes, drink from my wine glass. It will take a little steel to bend his will. But I am not a bag of bones sitting in front of an empty plate, not a jellyfish swishing about like an electric skirt. So I change the topic of conversation to how *loud* wind chimes can be, or the errant mosquito that got into the house last night and bit me *ten times,* and he shuts up immediately. He is interested in the outrages of history. I am the present, nervous and alert. Our eras do not overlap. There are years between us.

Small Talk

Because it is with strangers. Because strangers have reserves of sympathy that my family does not. Because my family thinks I'm silly. Because silly is not the point. Because the point is never to arrive at a point.

In Theory

So much on my mind, mostly ways to make Leo behave. The other day, Alexis asked me what I'd do if I didn't have Leo to worry about. Who I'd have been if I hadn't had to focus on him. "Should I factor you and Jason into this equation?" I asked. "No," she said. I shook my head—impossible—a mother cannot think this way. But something sent out a shoot. Movie producer? Taxidermist? Corny but fun to speculate. Teacher of night school classes? Taker of night school classes? The purposeful motions of creation: hammering shelves, planting seeds, carving woodblocks to stamp on Christmas cards. Or—aim higher, for god's sake—starting a press or penning a screenplay or nursing AIDS patients overseas. Alexis was waiting for me to speak. I didn't want to disappoint her, and so, of course, I did. "I can't stand to picture a past that doesn't involve you," I said. It wasn't even true. She said, "Mom, that's one hell of a failure of imagination." She paused. "I wanted to tell you I'm seeing a woman." "What's her name?" I asked, as if that would explain it. "Jess. Jessica. Let's keep it a secret from Dad." "Of course we will, of course we'll keep it a secret," I said. Knitting our hands together across the country.

Something Sweet

A woman comes out of an ice cream shop with a cup of ice cream, gets into her SUV, starts the engine, and sits there spooning stuff into her mouth. Ten minutes, fifteen. She's not waiting for anyone. Her windows are down and the car, the big car, is on. She eats evenly, without pleasure. Probably she has the air conditioning on too. Probably she's wearing aerobics clothes. Leo and I are standing out front with our cones. This woman is everything he hates, and I understand that. But he also hates nice things, like rationality and getting along with people. He holds his cone aloft and says, "I'd like to shove this in the bitch's face."

Mythologies

The true faces of dogs, eyes pricked red by the camera's light; the kids in the bath, slick and foamy; panoramas of beaches made impotent by distance; a pink stuffed turtle wearing a bowler hat; a box of rainbow chard at a farmers' market; Alexis holding her guinea pig to her chest; Teddy wearing sunglasses, jade beads, and the lean, complicit look of the sixties; Leo standing among his tomato plants proffering a cherry tomato; slurred row of elderly relatives; Jason in an open onesie squatting as if to defecate on the hood of the Dodge Dart; mountain goats with their shredded beards; me lighting one candle with another at Thanksgiving dinner (there's a gravy boat, a tray of rolls); an old boyfriend of Alexis's, his freckles like atolls; a pile of Jason's *Dungeons & Dragons* manuals, and (this must be why I took the picture) a piece of graph paper with the names of his avatars written on it: Hawk the Slayer. Vulcan the Pulverizer. Jason-of-the-Gunmetal-Fleece.

Exercise

Leo in the carport, warming up to go jogging. He strides back and forth, his arms swinging in staccato bursts at his sides. Back and forth. Concentrated. Doesn't seem to mind my and Alexis's giggling from the screen door. He's wearing his jogging outfit: swim trunks faded to pink. When he gets back he'll be dripping with sweat and stinking. Walk around the house all leisurely. And I'll shoo him upstairs to take a shower, but really I don't mind. His smell is honest, as is his pleasure after exercise. There are times when he's a machine that cannot be turned off, a thought that cannot be dismantled, a bellow that follows me around the house, but this isn't one of them. Bending now, doing toe touches and squats. He must have learned this regimen when he was on his high school's track team in Argostoli—he was a sprinter—something naïve and militaristic about it. He straightens up and pinwheels his arms, laughing at our laughter, and then he runs down the driveway and turns right onto the sidewalk and disappears behind a wall of green hedge. "I hope he doesn't see anyone I know," Alexis says.

Little Indignities

Alexis: "I can't believe that you used to have to wear a belt." Me: "What do you mean?" Alexis: "With your *pads.*" Me: "Oh. It's true." Alexis: "A belt. A pink plastic belt. It's barbaric." Me: "Are you menstruating?"

On "Little Indignities"

It's true that in the past I have asked my daughter if she's menstruating. Is that so bad? It wreaks havoc on one's mood, everyone knows that. Alexis thinks that she seeks solidarity with me but really she seeks to show me the error of my ways. That question about the belt was only to point out how leashed in I was, how chained. I was not supposed to calmly affirm its existence and then ask her about her own cycle. But isn't that a kind of rebellion, mother and daughter commiserating over their monthly thing? Not to her. Leaving the bloated cardboard shells of tampons floating in the toilet for Jason to find, maybe. Smudging the toilet paper roll with blood-stained fingers. The crime (of not getting pregnant—we exhort our girls to commit it) buried deep within her body, but the evidence out there for anyone to see.

Being

Bearing, braving, wanting, vying, paranoiding, neighboring,

fighting, underdressing, overdressing, shaking, drinking, to animals human characteristics attributing, assessing, accepting, if she's raising her children right wondering, why she said that thing regretting (though why *shouldn't* she have said that thing), beauty's keeping (sanctimonious apeing), beauty's leaving (the mystery of it happening), the stubborn push of the body's living, cooking, kissing, freedom impossible freedom.

Flight

I was nineteen, twenty, twenty-one. Now I'm forty-eight. I have to pee all the time. My arms thicken, my eyesight fuzzes, the spaces between my toes simmer and pop. Lying on my back, my chest is as flat as a boy's but still something beats beneath it that is distinctly female. It says, I'm-*here.* It says, It's-*me.* It doesn't know that its container has changed, that no one wonders about it anymore, or is interested in what it feels. But a teenager with a pea for a heart, now she's a force to be reckoned with! I sit in front of a mirror and brush my hair because I think messages may be transmitted to me there. A gesture that travels outside of time. But it's just me, brushing my hair, getting caught on the snags. A not-unpleasant looking me: rosebud mouth, pink cotton nightgown. Must I speak about sex? Must sex exist at all? Lately it's like . . . being trampled. It's like I was the site of a rally, and the crowd was excited and chanting slogans, and it felt good to care to really care about something, and then when the rally was over everyone just dropped their signs and water bottles and left, vamoosed, scuffing up the grass. The movement—the moment—already behind them. What happens to the field after the crowd has dispersed? What happens to the ground? A dandelion unbends its neck. A single feather drifts out of the sky from a bird I cannot see.

Nesting Dolls

The silence of a house after the children have departed: relief and regret and complication in it. Not any silence, one only you can hear. When Jason went off to college I still had Alexis. It was not unusual to find her napping on her single bed with her arms around her boyfriend's wormy waist, but still . . . "I'm sad that it ends here," I said when it was her turn to leave. I expected her to correct me. Instead, she looked at me with these eyes all done up in smoky liner and issued a statement like an ousted CEO: "I'm looking forward to spending time with new friends." What's with, I wondered, the pleasantries? This from a girl who always says exactly what she's thinking. Now I realize she was protecting herself. She didn't break up with her boyfriend until she arrived at college and saw all the other wormy waists. She didn't allow herself to care about a thing until she saw that other people did too. It's human. Her transformation to Portland lesbian was still years away. She even joined, for three months, a sorority. "They give you a plate with a donut on it, and on top of that a scoop of ice cream. No spoon, no fork. They wait to see what you'll do," she told me over the phone. "Well, what *do* you do?" I asked. "You do nothing," she said. "That's the trick. You do nothing." But it's not a trick, I thought. I'd hung up the phone and was sitting on the couch. Silence splintered into a clock's ticking.

Creation Story

He was disorienting, egotistical. I was disoriented, undone at the seams. He wasn't exactly chivalrous, but flattering in a way. I wasn't expecting chivalry, but was easily flattered. He took me to be a living representation of the place where he'd arrived. I was anything, anywhere, anyone wanted me to be. If I spun a globe and put my finger on a spot, I'd peek and do it over.

Going West

Days marked by nothing more than reflection, reading, walking. This was before the kids. Leo grew a beard that he'd scratch with nails kept a bit long for the purpose. The sound of the pages of his book turning sometimes overlapped with the sound of the pages of my book turning. Night fell like black snow against the windows. Everything that was outside was supposed to be outside, and everything that was inside was supposed to be inside. Trees had their mothers near. Couches had end tables. I was real for a while, able to intuit, think. I was a nice pair of antennae, cast from the rooftop above the clouds' lowest layers. White noise turned to gray. Other conversations, the logic of other people's days, had no power over me. Leo took coffee into the basement to write the book that would make his name (but never did). I cleaned coffee dribbles off the basement steps. Our happiness suddenly became manifest—I mean, when we became aware of it we had to move, because happiness is like a shove. We came out to California.

Shelter

After the guests left, the bride floated for a while above a table covered with half-eaten pieces of wedding cake and flower petals. Her face narrowed to a knotted chin, around which was tied a length of white ribbon.

Norman stood up and flicked her cheek, then cupped it more gently. "Come here," he said. But she rotated just as he tried to kiss her. "Is something wrong? Didn't you have fun tonight?"

She turned back to look at him. The smile that he'd drawn on her with lipstick was not a good indicator of how she felt. It was actually quite misleading.

"I've done this before, I admit. But this time it's going to be different," Norman said. "You're not like my exes, you're quiet. They were—how can I put this?—deluded by ideas of their own necessity. But not you, baby. Do you understand me?" He pulled on her ribbon and she bobbed vertiginously. "Is that a yes? Do I see a yes? Listen, you're my one and only. They might as well have never existed."

She remembered lying in the bin with the others. There was a red one with *Hip Hip Hooray* written on it, and a white one with *You Did It!* written on it, and she was plain yellow. She knew what they said though she could not see the letters until they were inflated. She knew the type—red was always *Hip Hip Hooray.* The feeling in the bin was of consequence and closeness. Then fingers lifted her and tugged at her nozzle, and she was filled with helium.

Norman tied her to his wrist and left the rented hall. He bounced along in his tuxedo shirt, bidding good evening to everyone who passed. There was greediness in his desire to engage, however briefly, with these scissor-legged beings. Her head hit the branch of a tree. "Oh god, sorry," he called. "My fault, my fault." She began to sink.

By the time they reached his apartment building, her head was even with his.

She had no bodily functions or fluids to speak of. He had chosen her especially because she was *not* human, but he'd hoped to discover some secret little compartment anyway. He knew to untie her—to create an opening—would be her demise, so that first night he made a wild grab for her and rubbed her with a swift, heretofore-unseen part of himself. There was a fuzzy sound, like the party store radio between stations. Suddenly she realized what he was doing. The songs had sung of this, something charged with electricity. Then he released her, and she bobbed to the far side of the room.

The next day, she was even with his shoulders. The next, his knees.

Now when they met each other in the hallway, the living room or kitchen, Norman made a show of sidestepping her, or bowing and extending his arm to indicate she should go first. He wanted her to know nothing, and everything, like a charming puzzle. He wanted her like a bauble, a child's toy. "I guess we'll just have to be friends," he said.

Finally she lay on the floor with the dust. One afternoon, while he slept on the couch, she skittered to his side. His face was lush, alive with dreams. *My girl,* he murmured, and she ducked beneath the couch. Next to her was a slim black box with pretty rows of buttons. "You too?" she asked. It said nothing.

She realized Norman had believed in her, if only briefly. Held against that, what was escape? And how would it even be done? A draft from the open window, perhaps—she cast her eye upon it, which shimmered like water made square. Then what? Flight had never interested her, though she knew some balloons who longed for nothing else. No, flight had been out of the question but she had landed anyway.

A Civilizing Effect

Edith told herself she wasn't going to date now that she was a grandmother, yet she'd gone ahead and moved in with a man named Pete. Pete suffered from a sleep disorder. He would appear to wake up in the middle of the night, talking and lecturing, singing sometimes. Once he even shuffled into the kitchen and pantomimed, wrist gracefully rotating, the scrambling of an egg. It was called confusional arousal, and after he was done he'd lie back down and close his eyes. In the morning, he'd say he couldn't remember anything.

She sat next to him as he watched a basketball game on TV. It was a warm evening in March. Edith paged through the newspaper, then turned to the television's antic screen. The players' legs were too long—three or four strides took them from one end of the glossy court to the other, where they would converge, shoes squealing. And if the athletes were getting taller, as she'd read somewhere, shouldn't the height of the basket be raised? She'd also read that they used to play the game with peach baskets. She imagined advertisers stamping their names across the slatted wooden sides.

"Pete," she said, "you know what would be funny?" He

raised his finger in a shushing motion, bobbing it up and down to indicate that, while he requested silence, he did so temporarily. Edith left the couch for the bedroom and undressed to her underwear and a white T-shirt with armpits the color of tea stains. She wasn't trying as hard with him as she had with other men. She didn't have the nerves, the giddy quick shakes, not a bit of it. She didn't even have a sense of propriety. The music of a commercial began and as Pete walked into the room she scratched freely between her toes with a pencil. "I don't have any paper, so help me remember what we need from the grocery," she said. "Milk, pineapple, and scallions." She patted the bed. He sat down. "And cheddar cheese. Milk, pineapple, scallions, and cheddar cheese."

Pete had been an engineer for twenty-five years with General Electric. He wore a short sleeved button-up shirt decorated with GE's curly insignia, which looked to Edith like a bird doubled over and cleaning itself. "I won't be with you at the store, so what good is it to tell me?" he said.

"It helps to hear it out loud," Edith said.

Pete shook his head. He had neck fat, not a disgusting amount but some. Wearing goggles, looking down at a circuit panel, his chin would fold into his neck twice, that was all.

She moved her bare legs under the sheets. I'm splayed out in this man's bed, she thought. This man has pressed his nether part up, up, inside me! She thought of her insides as beautifully functional as a microwave or a telephone or any other device she depended on and whose mechanics she was utterly disinterested in deciphering. She thought, This man has made guttural acquiescent sounds especially for me. A universal yes, a moan. An okay cloaked in darkness. And to those sounds I have added my own. She wanted to scandalize herself but it wasn't working. She didn't know Pete all that well, but how could she? She was fifty-five, past the point in her life when she could be worshipful and receptive. Everything, everyone was changing. Her daughter had her own baby now, a boy born prematurely and called Titan. When Edith met friends for dinner, she found herself imagining her parking stub back in the car. What was it doing? Did it miss queuing in the machine with the other stubs? When she had wine, she wanted water. When she took a bite of fish, she craved cucumber salad with a little dill.

"I know it's silly," she said now to Pete. "Wouldn't you like to travel, since you're retired? I'd like to possess a fine object from another country."

"What about your career?" Pete asked considerately. Edith hardly had a career—she was a part-time bank teller.

"Oh, anyone can dispense cash," she said, waving her hand. "I'd like a Black Forest cuckoo clock. Or a mantilla."

The next day, after working a morning shift, Edith stopped by the grocery store. As she entered the massive building she promptly forgot one of the items. "Milk, scallions, cheddar cheese," she kept repeating, as if the missing thing would fall unbeknownst to her in place. She pushed her cart rapidly. She was distracted, she was at that hand-wringing place, that seat on the departing plane. A list would have saved her but she'd had no paper, no precious goddamn paper. As she turned into the cereal aisle, she rear-ended a cart with a toddler in it, causing his head to flop back and then forwards, where it lolled, blonde bangs like silken lampshade fringe.

"Gid!" his mother said. She dropped the box of cereal she was holding, which Edith picked up. The cereal was supposed to look and taste like little peanut butter-and-jelly sandwiches. It even came with crusts. The thought that perhaps she and Pete could share a bowl of this grotesque stuff calmed Edith. She would put a spoonful of it into his mouth, she would feed him, a motion she hadn't made since her daughter was an infant. She recalled that her hand, as she held out the spoon, used to shake.

"I think Gideon needs an apology," the mother said. Gideon lifted his head and regarded Edith with, it seemed to her, extreme disinterest.

"I'm sorry you were in my way," Edith said. Was she fifty-five? She felt glorious, she felt forty. She turned to the mother. "Was Gideon regulation size when he was born?"

"He was quite large."

"You're lucky."

The mother balanced a bag of tortilla chips on the boy's head and he giggled. "I know."

"Your luck," Edith said, "or your knowledge of your luck, will invariably wane."

"I know that too," the mother said.

Edith looked steadily at her—red ponytail, intransigent chin—and she returned Edith's gaze. Edith blinked. The woman blinked. Edith adjusted her left bra strap. The woman did the same. Edith became impatient with their little game, remembered—pineapple—and trotted away.

When she got home, Pete was napping. She was riffling through a kitchen drawer for her reading glasses when she heard him say, "A sign of hospitality." She turned around to see him pointing to the pineapple on the counter. His hair was mashed to the side of his head and his eyes were averted. He was sleepwalking, he was becoming more and more agile. "The Carib Indians called it 'anana,' or 'excellent fruit.' In the 1600s, it remained so uncommon a treat that King Charles II of England posed for a portrait receiving a pineapple as a gift."

Edith didn't move. She'd done some research on confusional arousal and she knew that attempting to wake Pete would be a mistake. It would stymie the two sides of his brain even more, the part that controlled simple motor reflexes being convinced it was awake and the part that reasoned and recognized the effect of his actions still asleep. The best thing to do was simply to go along with what he was saying. She didn't want his mind to become locked in place.

Pete sat down at the dining room table. "I'm so hungry," he announced helplessly, as if he didn't really expect to get anything to eat. He plucked a pair of candles from their holders and began to rap them on the table. "To-by, To-by, To-by. We were in college together, long ago. At the Hyacinth Mixer, everyone gathered round him and made him play the drums. He was a good drummer, but he hated performing. His face turned crimson. Later that night, he died in a car accident."

Edith gasped. It was unconscionable. After hounding and embarrassment, Toby didn't deserve to die, he deserved to be taken out for ice cream. The world's injustice was always there, but it was usually obligingly invisible.

Pete gestured again to the pineapple. "May I have some?" As Edith peeled and cored the unwieldy fruit she wondered if he would wake with a full stomach, or if the food he consumed during his episodes was phantom food, drifting and non-nourishing. She wondered if he saw her—Edith, his new girlfriend, tall and thin with hair like pillow stuffing—or if she was to him a specter in a dream, a fuzzy whatever-he-concocted-her-to-be. She placed the pineapple in front of him and he consumed it steadily with both hands, alternating right, left, taking rhythmic bites. He licked his lips. "Tingles," he said, and got up from the table and headed back to the bedroom.

She listened for the door to close and sat down. She was a grandmother. Of a preemie, of Titan. When he was still in the incubator she would visit the hospital with her daughter Cassandra, and after they were done hovering over him, marveling at him, everything miniaturized like an architect's model of a building, after they were done holding him—the weight of a few beanbags—in their hands, they would wander the corridors until they were ready to visit him again. Did Cassandra hope, returning to Titan after an absence of even forty-five minutes, that he'd have grown a little? Her face was always peaceful upon seeing him. Edith was the one who was disappointed that her daughter had not produced a larger baby. Titan was cute, in his own way—he looked like a small and deeply concentrated monk, body shriveled beyond need, beyond the reach of anything physical. But she wanted to be able to take him home and put him in a baby swing with three or four different motorized settings. She wanted to see how he looked in the onesie patterned with whales she'd purchased for him, and to place a hat on his head without it swallowing him up. The day Titan was born, she'd asked the doctor why he had arrived so early and the doctor had said, "Because he was getting bored in there? Believe me, I wish I knew."

Edith and Cassandra walked. The hospital had its own collection of art, black-and-white photographs of household items: a box of detergent, a spatula, an iron with a stout and wrinkled cord. It had a library in which Edith located a copy of Dudley Steibling's *Grotesqueries,* a mystery she'd been wanting to read. (The library loaned books to hospital patients only, so Cassandra checked it out under Titan's name and the book had been delivered by chute to the neonatal intensive care ward.) On the top floor was a museum that displayed Civil War–era prostheses, wooden with leather straps and hinges; and on the rooftop a café with a wonderful hearts of palm salad.

Now, two months later, with Titan safely at home, Cassandra was busy breastfeeding and burping him, changing diapers the size of cocktail napkins and applying ointment to his rashes. Edith thought that she must have some qualms, that motherhood was a complexity, a convolution, to which her daughter was surely not immune, but Cassandra claimed she was enjoying every minute of it. She was unmarried and the father was a local boy whom Edith wanted to confront the way she wanted to know what was going on in Pete's head during one of his arousals—avidly, avidly. Cassandra was living in Edith's old apartment, which she'd left furnished. She dialed the number now.

"What's Titan doing?" she asked when her daughter answered the phone.

"He's just lying here. He looks like an apricot."

"Pete had another episode. He had historical things to say about the pineapple."

"Mom, you need to take him to see someone. He might be hallucinating, not getting enough oxygen."

"Why don't you and Titan come over for dinner?" Edith asked.

Hanging up the phone, she was struck by how odd it was to invite her own daughter to dinner. This person with whom she used to spend every minute—waking and sleeping—now accepted or rejected her overtures casually, without a hint of how unnatural a *no* could seem. But Cassandra had said yes this time, and for that Edith was grateful.

Later that night, lying in bed next to Pete, Edith could still smell Titan's powdery scent on her hands. She'd glimpsed his tongue as he cried, rippling in the dark back of his mouth. His cry was astonishing. It was like a pail of water tossed against a window—a splash of sound, a dripping and rolling down—and when it was gone it left the room cleaner. Then Cassandra nursed him and he became lost in the folds of her shirt, only his twiggy shins and feet visible. She had told Edith that when she fed Titan at home, sitting in Edith's recliner in the corner of the living room, she stared at the lights in other people's apartments and watched for a flash, a sliver of their occupants. She said it made her feel lonely, that she could no longer enter those bright places herself. Edith knew whose apartments she meant. The Goodwins', the Clovers'. Lights on at all hours, people coming and going, the feather-tip of laughter in the air. Ease and malaise, Edith thought when she thought of those people. You don't want to go near any of them, she'd had the impulse to say to her daughter, but remained silent. It wasn't that Cassandra coveted their company, she understood this.

She lay in the dark, unfamiliar room. She was sure that when she got up to go to the bathroom in the middle of the night she'd stumble over Pete's pants, gap-waisted on the floor with the belt still coiled through the loops. She was marooned, she was badly stationed. It had been her choice to move in with Pete, a choice that had corresponded with Titan's birth, compensated for it somehow.

Pete rolled onto his back. She raised herself on her elbow and stared down into his face. His eyelashes looked blotted out.

"Edith?" Pete said.

"Yes."

He didn't turn to her. "Cassandra and Titan were here? We ate?"

"Are you awake?"

"Negative, I think."

"Do you know what you're saying?" Edith asked.

His lids fluttered. "Would you like to make love to me?"

"We could try . . . we could see." Pete began to untie the string waist of his pajama bottoms. "Kiss me first," Edith said.

He reared up in bed with startling speed and found her face with both hands. His kiss missed her lips and landed on her chin. He attempted to pull her T-shirt off by yanking down on the fabric.

"Other way," Edith said. "Up, up."

Pete reached into a drawer of the bedside table, brought out a pair of scissors, and began to cut her shirt in half. Edith let him do it, tensing her stomach so one of its rolls of flesh would disappear. He cut expertly all the way up to the neckline, and her shirt slipped off her shoulders.

"This is quite daring," she said.

"Would you like me to go all the way down?" Pete asked, indicating the gray sweat shorts she was wearing.

Edith shook her head and slipped out of her shorts. The veins in her legs were long and alarmingly visible. Pete positioned himself over her as if he were about to do a push-up and began to kiss her neck and the top part of her chest. His lips felt cool and dark and wet, as if he were stamping her with black ink. Then he looked up with a puzzled expression on his face. "I can't do it."

"Why not?" She was just beginning to enjoy herself.

"I'm not here!"

"You're here," she said.

"You may be experiencing me, but I'm not experiencing myself."

"Fight it."

"I don't know how." He curled back into the shallow indentation his body had left in the mattress.

"You have to stay still, resist the exertion, deeply dream."

"I haven't dreamed in years."

"You have to have something to dream about," Edith said gently. She began smoothing back his curly hair, which coupled with his high forehead reminded her of a wooden clown face she'd hung long ago in the kitchen of her apartment. The clown had a peg for a nose and beneath its smiling visage was a poem:

While you wash the dishes
While you wash the clothes
Your rings will be safe
Hanging here on my nose.

She'd used it dutifully despite its banal assumptions about chores (who hand-washed clothes?), and now when she did the dishes in Pete's kitchen she never knew quite what to do with her jewelry. She didn't have anything very expensive, but to feel her rings sliding around on her sudsy fingers was unnerving.

She went into the bathroom to get her robe and stood looking in the mirror. Her breasts were medium-sized and widely spaced and had not for a long time been the object of anyone's adoration. They were soft, inert. Her nipples looked like trammeled acorns. It seemed unfair to see her body compromised so. She flipped the switch and the bathroom became dark again. Light in the middle of the night was always a mistake.

Downstairs, she dialed her old number. "How did Pete seem tonight?" she asked when Cassandra picked up the phone.

"Fine," Cassandra said. "His chicken was good. I like all that lemon and oregano."

"He can cook for sure."

"It's late, Mom. Titan just fell back to sleep."

"Take his father to court, Cassandra. Establish paternity."

"I have no need to."

"Do you still see him?"

"Sometimes. He brings money."

Edith imagined the baleful local boy stealing something,

pawning it, and bringing Cassandra a bunch of crumpled dollar bills. "Good," she said. "He owes you."

"He owes Titan," Cassandra said. "Titan's owed the world."

"I'm going to do my best for him. He'll have music lessons if he wants. Wrestling matches. A second language," Edith said.

"Maybe he won't want those things. Maybe he'll want to learn to sail."

"Does his father sail?"

"Of course not," Cassandra said.

"Is he tender toward Titan?"

"He makes gobbling sounds and pretends to eat his fist."

Edith paused. Titan's father wore baggy pants and T-shirts printed with incendiary messages. His hair sprang chaotically from his head. Did he really know how to be playful? He was too demonstratively quiet, too ominous and judging. What had attracted him to Cassandra? Her daughter's features were petite, like a couple of pennies on a plate. Her hair was dark again because she didn't want to use dye while she was breastfeeding.

"I have something I want to tell you. I regret any false enthusiasm I might have displayed toward you as a child, any egging on of foolish games that I encouraged simply to occupy you. I wish I had always been properly impressed."

"It's hard to be impressed with the same thing over and over again," Cassandra said.

"You were constantly changing."

"But the request was the same. Look at me, look at me, look at me."

"I miss your youth," Edith said.

She lay on the couch after she'd hung up the phone, doing leg lifts. It wasn't entirely true that she missed Cassandra's youth, though that was the best way she could have said it. It was the potential, all the rangy possibility that her daughter had possessed and then discarded, not knowing what she was throwing away. That which was available to Cassandra only once, seeing her move beyond it, was the source of Edith's nostalgia. She sighed and began to lift her arms too, so she wouldn't strengthen disproportionately just one part of her body.

She woke the following morning to the sound of Pete making coffee. The slippery material of her robe was shot through with wrinkles that disappeared when she stood and re-formed when she sat back down.

"You attempted to seduce me while you were asleep," Edith said when Pete came into the living room.

"But," Pete said, "how did I . . . ?"

"Admirably," she said.

"It was good, or?"

"Hell yeah."

His face twitched. "How much was crescendo, and how much . . . ?"

"The quick, the marrow?"

"Oh, I don't want to know," Pete said.

"These things are best left unsaid," Edith agreed.

"Here." Pete thrust his coffee cup at her. "I'm going to take a shower." He disappeared into the bathroom.

She took a sip. The coffee tasted like medicated mud,

though if he asked she'd probably say it was fine. She wondered how many times in her life she'd lied. Hundreds? Thousands? She had once been married and had lied to her husband about how he looked in certain items of clothing (a Bolero tie, a pair of striped overalls), how his breakfast hash tasted, and he'd left her anyway. He'd carved his intentions into a blonde-wood coffee table: *VACATING LOWER 48*. This had taken the length of the table and some effort, she was sure. The only satisfaction she felt when she returned home and found the message was in imagining how much longer the carving had taken him than he'd expected, and how, after he'd begun, he figured he couldn't abandon the job halfway. He'd have grown frustrated with his own dumb ambition, when he could have left her a regular pen and paper note. She'd pictured him in his rattling pickup truck on his way to Seattle, flexing the fingers that had gripped the pocketknife for so long. She'd lied to old boyfriends about how it felt when they touched her, running their fingers over her in vehement, searching strokes, the theory, she supposed, being that if they covered enough territory they would hit upon the proper spot and release a mini-lightening bolt inside her, a clap of euphoria. She'd lied to Cassandra mostly by encouraging her to do her chemistry homework and practice the French horn, as if those things would figure in her future at all. The only people she didn't lie to regularly, she realized, were her customers at the bank. She didn't add dollars to their account balances where there were none, though they might have appreciated it, temporarily.

And how often was she lied to? Hadn't a look of queasy acquiescence come over Pete's face when she asked him recently if he liked a pair of her earrings that were shaped like parakeets? But it didn't matter. She preferred it that way. Lies were better than evasions.

The water was still running. Edith figured she'd take the last part of Pete's shower with him. She opened the bathroom door to a wall of steam. The toilet lid was down, and Pete was sitting on it.

"You're dry," Edith said.

"I just came in here," Pete answered.

"To?"

Pete shrugged. "Your implication was making me nervous."

"That something happened between us last night while you were sleeping?" Edith's face grew hot. "Well, it started to."

"That's better," Pete answered. "I'm not so lost that you can tell me anything."

"I'm sorry."

Pete reached over and adjusted the water temperature. The hair on his forearm glistened with drops when he pulled it back. "I can't get this hot enough. I was going to try to scald my arm."

"Scald your arm!"

"I figured it would keep me awake."

"Well, your hot water heater must be set to a reasonable temperature," she said, "thank goodness."

"But I decided," Pete said, standing up, "that there are so many different kinds of pain, and just as many remedies. It doesn't seem worth it."

He left the room, shutting the door behind him. Edith turned the shower off. She stared at her feet on the natty rug and felt, suddenly, very sad. The sadness was stirred up by Pete but he was not the source of it. She had to go to her job at the bank and manipulate currency. A dollar bill carried an infinitesimal number of germs on its surface, and change, who knew what happened to change before it was collected from beneath sofa cushions and the sweaty soles of feet? She put on a blue linen skirt and brushed her teeth. She wanted to call Cassandra but knew that she shouldn't. Her daughter was a mother now, which made her less of a daughter. The only other person in the world who remembered Cassandra the way she did was her ex-husband, the one who'd left for Alaska to become a trapper when Cassandra was eight. He scented antelope meat with sesame oil, which the wolves apparently loved. Antelope meat, ragged pungent hunks of it. Edith could not even make a guess if he killed the antelope himself, she knew him so little. Back when they were together, twenty years ago, she would have said no. *No,* he said, his eyes widening, when she told him she was pregnant. But they'd gotten married and things had been troubled and still she hadn't wanted him to leave. He'd also said, shortly before the end, "You haven't had a civilizing effect on me," as if there existed in men a special, tangled kind of wilderness that women were bound to unknot.

Edith got in her car and drove to the bank. She was opening today and had to use four different keys to unlock the front doors, each slightly larger than the one before. Walking past the rows of vaults, she realized she no longer wondered what was in them. Other people's possessions—jewelry, photographs of pallid-faced ancestors, paperwork that made lives official—didn't interest her anymore. She was just as blasé about the things in her apartment, though she knew that her daughter was now their caretaker. Sometimes she missed her colander, handsome and tin, whose striations made the pattern of a star. She thought again of Cassandra sitting in her recliner, staring out the window at the lights in the other apartments, their frivolous shine. Feeding Titan for the tenth, eleventh time. What sort of dinner did she make for herself? A bowl of cereal, plain spaghetti? The night's riches dripping through the fingers of the trees.

She worked the drive-through while Yolanda, her co-worker, tended the counter. "Pardon me, ma'am," a fuzzy voice said through the intercom. Looking up, she saw Pete driving Cassandra's car with Titan in the back strapped into his infant seat.

"What are you doing?" Edith asked.

"Cassandra is napping at our place. I'm giving her a break."

"Oh, that's nice."

He revved the engine. "I'm the master of this little guy's fate. I'm completely in charge of him."

Edith's heart pounded once, hard. "You've got to be careful," she said.

"We're having breakfast out. I need money."

She withdrew twenty-five dollars from Pete's account and passed it to him through the sliding tray. "One of Titan's socks has slipped off," she said.

"I can't hear you."

Edith leaned closer to the little microphone. "His foot is bare," she said, pointing.

Pete waved his hand. "A baby foot isn't meant to be all dressed up."

Edith felt like she had in the grocery store the other morning—a quickening sense of departure, a departure come too soon. She took a deep breath. "Are you going to that new pancake place?" she asked.

Pete put the money in his wallet and revved the engine again. "I am really quite normal," he said. "I've got inner equilibrium."

"Not many people do," Edith said. Titan, who had been asleep, opened his eyes.

"Then I'm abnormal."

"Not abnormal, just lucky," she said desperately.

"My dear, don't try to pacify me. Titan and I are going to dine."

"He'll get hungry. What will you give him if he cries?"

"Mother's milk." Pete patted a quilted diaper bag that sat on the passenger's seat. As if on cue, Titan began to wail.

"Gotta go," Pete said.

"Take him home!" Edith said shrilly. Titan cocked his head to the side and palpated his neck with his little hands. He was wearing jeans that buttoned all the way up the inside of both legs, like chaps.

"I feel something like pity for you," Pete said.

"Don't say that."

"Pity and love, pitiful love." He pulled away, the ragged end of the baby's cry trailing out of the car window.

Edith's heart was pounding steadily now. She switched the green OPEN light to a red CLOSED, and ran outside. The street was empty. The car was gone. Cassandra was sleeping in. It was as if Titan had never been born. If Titan had never been born, that might mean Cassandra didn't exist. And if Cassandra didn't exist, Edith may never have met her ex-husband, may never have moved to this midwestern college town to get her accounting degree. Who would she be back in Virginia, which was where she came from? A dot, a pinprick. Piece of gravel, gritty cubic inch of soil. Anything whose beauty resided in its utter placidity. She went back inside and dispensed suckers to a couple of teenagers who were much too old for them.

She spent her lunch break squatted on the curb in front of the bank. At 11:45, Pete drove by very quickly, his tires whining. A few minutes later he whipped past in the other direction. Edith knew he was asking her for something, and her answer was her unchanging posture on the curb. If a request is refused, she wondered, does that make the asking more ardent? Titan needs his mother, she thought. She stepped into the middle of the street.

The next day, she sat on the couch with her foot in a cast. After Pete had run over it he'd continued to drive several yards, then stopped and opened his door and stuck out his head to see if she'd fallen. She had. He reversed to her with the door still open and picked her up off the ground. She'd wanted to pummel his head with her fists. Instead, she leaned against him as if he were her only witness to the strange and cruel act that had just befallen her. When he placed her in the car she saw that the infant seat was empty, the padding thin. Was it used, had the local boy ripped it out of some other mother's car? Her head lolled. The pain in her foot was hot and still, like something metal. "I'm sorry, you appeared out of nowhere," Pete kept repeating until the words got scrambled up in her mind and she heard *Out of nowhere I'm sorry you appeared.* "Where's Titan," she asked, "where's Titan?" "With Cassandra," he said.

Pete was napping now. Edith sipped some orange juice. The second hand of the clock above the mantel didn't appear to move yet she heard its small motor sweeping it forward. The numbers were delicately curved, calligraphic. Twelve minutes passed before he appeared and sat down next to her.

"You're asleep, of course," she said flatly.

Pete nodded his head.

"Here's my quandary. If I tell you now that I'm leaving, you won't remember that I said so. One day I'll just be gone."

"That would be a shock."

"But if I tell you when you're awake, you'll worry and feel bad."

"Then don't go," Pete said.

She considered not going, and going, and neither alternative provided her with a place to be. Where did women her age spend their time? Was there an enclave, a lyceum? A plaza equipped with pillows and snacks, ringing with debate?

"My foot itches," she said.

"Can I sign your cast?"

She nodded. Pete walked over to the desk and returned with a pen. He wrote *For Edith* across the rough plaster. "Your name belongs here," he said.

"It *is* mine, isn't it?" Edith looked down at the crude L of the cast. She had to wear it for six weeks and then the young doctor at the hospital would saw through it. When Pete cut her shirt in half it was the suddenness of the gesture that made it tender. An unconsidered thing. A brave motion.

Acknowledgments

I'd like to thank the editors of the following journals in which these stories first appeared:

"My Escapee" in *Tin House;* "A Civilizing Effect" in *A Public Space;* "Celebrants" in *McSweeney's;* "The Help" (as "Chief of Nurses") in *Epoch;* "Sink Home" in *Green Mountains Review;* "Examination" in *The Gettysburg Review;* "Privations" in *The Cincinnati Review;* "Shelter" in *Quick Fiction;* "Posthumous Fragments of Veronica Penn" in *The Collagist* and *The Milan Review.*

I'd like to thank Julie Paegle, Jessica Lewis Luck, Kelly Pender, Matthew Vollmer, Nic and Abby Brown, Austin Bunn, Sarah Cowgill, Midori Baer, Gabi Grannis, Kirsten Suttner, Erin McConnell, Muna Hussein, Sorrel Stielstra, Amy Barrett, and Renee Zuckerbrot for their friendship and good counsel, and Evaggelos, Crista, and Mark Vallianatos for their support.

Thank you to the MacDowell Colony; Lisel Ashlock; Nicole Belle; Bruce Wilcox, Sally Nichols, and the University of Massachusetts Press; the Association of Writers and Writing Programs; and especially Jhumpa Lahiri.

And to Kevin Moffett, for writing stories in the first place.